# TEXAS LAWMAN

# TEXAS LAWMAN

## Ray Hogan

SAGEBRUSH
Large Print Westerns

Copyright © 1967 by Ray Hogan

First published in Great Britain by ISIS Publishing Ltd
First published in the United States by Lancer Books

Published in Large Print 2008 by ISIS Publishing Ltd.,
7 Centremead, Osney Mead, Oxford OX2 0ES
United Kingdom
by arrangement with
Golden West Literary Agency

**British Library Cataloguing in Publication Data**
Hogan, Ray, 1908–
    Texas Lawman. – Large print ed. –
    (Sagebrush western series)
    1. Western stories
    2. Large type books
    I. Title
    813.5'4 [FS]

ISBN 978–0–7531–8016–7 (hb)

Printed and bound in Great Britain by
T. J. International Ltd., Padstow, Cornwall

# CHAPTER
# ONE

Comanches! . . . They were out there — somewhere.

Dan Ricker sprawled in the thin shadow of a manzanita and searched the sun-blasted land below with patient eyes. From where he lay, just beneath the rim of a ragged hogback, he could see for miles. There was nothing but the endless stretches of glittering sand and rock, thirsting cedars, grotesque chollas, and starved snakeweed.

He scowled and swore deeply as fresh sweat cut runnels through the gray dust clothing his face. Three days now — three days of no water, little food, and brief rest while the lean copper warriors dogged his trail. He had tried all the tricks in his bag, and nothing had worked. Late that morning he had swung into a brushy draw gashed in the body of a towering butte, desperate, knowing it was his only hope. He had hidden his sorrel as best he could in a tangle of greasewood and saltbush, and crawled to a point where he could watch the slope below. Now he waited, like a dark, gray-eyed wolf at bay.

It had been hell. The Comanches had jumped him shortly after daybreak three days past. A small raiding party had taken him unawares. During the quick,

1

violent fight he had lost rifle and canteen. There had been no opportunity of recovering either, although he had given a good account of himself with his pistol.

He had managed to get away, and since then it had been a deadly game of hide-and-seek while he whipped back and forth trying to shake the Comanches. In so doing he had lost his precise bearings and he now had no exact idea of where he was — only that he was somewhere in the wasted desolation of southwest Texas.

"All right — you lousy guteaters!" he croaked into the blistering silence. "Come on!"

He shifted on the hot sand, laid his gun on a flat rock in front of him, and wiped at the sweat misting his eyes. If he had to die, it might as well be here. A bullet would even be better than dying of thirst out on the endless mesas — and that's what he faced if he managed to survive the Comanches. He could get along without the rifle but no man traveled that Godforsaken cauldron of loneliness without water.

He reached up, dug into his shirt pocket for tobacco and papers, thought better of it. The smell of cigarette smoke could be a giveaway. He swore softly, then relaxed and again wiped at the sweat clothing his bearded face. If he got out of this Goddamn mess . . .

His thoughts came to a dead standstill. He froze. Below, at the base of the draw, an Indian had moved suddenly into view, dark head tipped down as he searched the ground for tracks. Ricker grinned tightly. There had been a rocky bench there. When he turned off he had paused and taken the precaution of wiping out the sorrel's hoofprints with a clump of creosote bush. The Comanches were having trouble; they couldn't figure out which direction he had taken when he moved off the bench.

He slid his hand forward and picked up his pistol. It was hot to his touch, and for several moments he held it loosely. Below, a second Comanche came into sight and halted beside the first. He said something, dropped from his pony, and hunched down over the trail, studying the gravel. Sweat glistened on his bowed back, and sunlight glinted dully off his black hair. A third Comanche appeared . . . a fourth . . . and then all seven of the party who had jumped him were below.

Ricker calculated the odds. If they came up the draw in a body he stood a good chance of getting three or four of them before his gun was empty — but it wasn't likely they would do it that way. They would scatter and work upslope singly, winding in and out of the brush and rock. He'd be hard pressed to hold his own against them. He might get off two or three shots, and then they would be swarming in from all sides.

He grinned again at the prospect. He'd give the bastards hell while he could. And they'd have to kill him; he wasn't about to let them capture him and sell him to the Comancheros. Anything beat slavery in the mines of Mexico.

Ricker's fingers tightened about the butt of his revolver. The brave who had been examining the trail was getting to his feet. He stood for several moments staring up at the butte, then swung his glance to the north as though still uncertain of the course Ricker had followed.

Abruptly he turned to his horse and vaulted onto its back. Hope lifting slowly within him, Dan watched as the Comanche thrust his feet into the rope that encircled his pony's belly to form crude stirrups. The brave said something to the others. All looked upslope. Dan lay motionless, staring back into their dark, fierce faces while his breath hung in his throat. For a time it seemed to him that their eyes were directly on him. And then he realized they looked not at him, but above him, to the crest of the butte beyond.

He forced himself to remain absolutely motionless on the hot sand. The slightest move on his part could catch their attention. Sudden worry caught at him. The sorrel was back there, behind him. Had the big gelding stirred, attracted them? Was it the sorrel they looked at rather than the rim?

Sweat trickled down his face, crept under his collar, ran onto his chest. His body ached from its tense, rigid position, and the sun's driving lances caused his skin to prickle. Gnats buzzed about him continuously, annoying his ears, nose, and mouth. His throat was paper-dry, and his dust-rimmed, bloodshot eyes smarted from the glare.

The urge possessed him to leap to his feet, to go charging down the slope shooting as he ran — to get it over with. But the instinctive animal determination to stay alive overrode the wild impulse, and he hung on.

The moments dragged by. A whip-tailed lizard emerged from a crevice in the rocks and halted only inches from Ricker's hand, observing him from beady eyes black as anthracite. The sun's drive cut into him. His jaws opened and he began to pant.

At the foot of the arroyo there was sudden commotion. Moving only his eyes Ricker saw one of the Comanches, evidently their chief, knee his horse to the front of the group. He was a lithe, half-bent copper figure wearing only a ragged, dirty loincloth, soft leather moccasins, and a battered, crumpled-brimmed old army campaign hat.

He said something, the sound but not the words carrying up to Ricker. He made an imperious gesture toward the north and rode off the ledge. The remaining braves stared after him briefly, then followed. Evidently they were in disagreement as to where Ricker had gone; the young chief had finally broken the deadlock by deciding the butte was not the answer and riding on.

Relief poured through Dan. He released his taut muscles, allowing himself to settle flat on the sand. The lizard scurried back into the crevice. The gnats, disturbed, buzzed and pulled off in a thin cloud.

Ricker, tension eased, raised his head carefully. The Comanches were two hundred yards away, moving in single file along the base of the talus. The brave with the campaign hat was in the lead. He was still hunched forward on his pony with the sunlight glistening on patches of sweat that lay on his back.

Ricker lay quiet, watched them dwindle into the distance and disappear. He rose then and, unconsciously cautious, made his way to the sorrel. The big horse had blown himself out and was now breathing normally after the hard run. Ricker went to the saddle, grunting wearily when his seat hit the saddle.

He moved off down the wash at a slow walk, letting the gelding pick his own way down the grade while he studied the flats and rolling hillocks that lay ahead. He had one thing in mind — get away from the butte as fast as possible. The Comanches had overlooked him once — but they would continue to search, and the second time he might not be so fortunate.

He was quartering the sun. To his left would be Mexico and the much-needed water of the Rio Grande. Both were several days distant, and he knew that neither he nor the sorrel could last the journey. Straight ahead would lie New Mexico. That was his best bet. His chances for running onto a ranch or a homestead were far better. He might even locate a spring or a creek, if he could hold out until he reached the higher mountains looming vaguely, like coils of blue-gray smoke, in the west. Ricker glanced at the fireball hanging motionless overhead in a cloudless arch of blue. If he could hold out . . .

He rode on, breaking out of the wash onto the rocky shelf, dipping again into a lower arroyo. It would be smart to keep to the gullies and depressions, where he could not be seen by the Comanches should they decide to double back. Indians were always unpredictable. They could be counted on to do the unexpected.

A cholla grazed his hand, and he jerked away, cursing softly. At that moment a faint smoke plume twisting lazily up from the horizon to the north seized his attention. He pulled the sorrel to a halt and stared. A grin pulled at his cracked lips and he winced at the pain. Smoke meant a town — or possibly a ranch or homestead. In any event he would find water and food.

Ricker touched the gelding with his spurs, eager to move on. Again he pulled up. Far below on the floor of the swale ahead two riders appeared. They had emerged from behind a swelling in the land that hid them from sight. They were following a narrow band of brush that traced crookedly along the low point of the hollow. They rode side by side, one on a huge black horse whose coat glistened in the bright sun, the other on a chunky buckskin. Evidently, they too were pointing for the distant smoke column.

Dan studied them with narrow, hopeful interest. He saw the two men glance toward him, their faces only shadowy, indistinct blurs, and continue on, not breaking pace. The trail they rode dropped into another cup, and they vanished from view. They would appear again a quarter mile farther on, Ricker saw.

They would have water, and the thought of that moved Dan to action. Leaning forward, he sent the sorrel downslope at a trot, but wise to the ways of men in the vast, lonely stretches of the frontier, he made no secret of his intentions and kept well in the open.

He reached the foot of the grade, then angled for the end of the brush where he judged the pair would break out. He saw then that it was an old, seldom-traveled road they pursued, and he felt a vague surprise at the discovery.

He drew the sorrel to a stop and listened into the hot stillness. He could hear no sound of the riders — no dry rasp of brush against leather, no thud of horses' hooves; there was only the grating clack of insects in the burned-off grass and the faraway and lonely cooing of a mourning dove. Ricker frowned. The trail must have swung wide through the tangle of mesquite and other scrub growth. It was taking the men longer than he had figured.

It made no difference. The road lay directly ahead and in plain view. They would have to appear if they planned to follow it on northward. He swallowed, tried to ease his craving throat, clung to his patience.

Moments passed, and then he heard their approach. He touched the sorrel with his spurs. Might as well wait on the road. A quiet motion at the edge of the opening in the brush caught his eye. He halted. The man on the buckskin rode into the sunlight. A lawman's star glinted on his breast. The hammer of the pistol he held in his right hand was at full cock.

"Close enough, mister," the lawman said in a flat, nasal voice. "Just set right where you are."

# CHAPTER
# TWO

Dan Ricker lifted his hands slowly. Anger plucked at his nerves, pulling the corners of his mouth into hard angles.

"You're mighty all-fired jumpy," he said in a rough voice. "All I'm looking for is a drink of water."

The lawman studied him through metallic blue eyes. He was an old man, well up in his sixties. He wore his gray hair shoulder length, matched it with a flowing mustache that curved downward in a smooth crescent below a beaklike nose. Authority and unyielding pride rode his squareset shoulders like an eagle.

"Maybe so," he said, his expression not changing. "Who are you?"

Dan returned the lawman's pushing stare. "Why? Some reason you ought to know?"

"There is. What do they call you?"

The tall rider shrugged. "Ricker," he said, relenting. "Dan Ricker."

"Headin' for where?"

Ricker considered that. "Can't see as that's any of your business either, but I'm aimed for Oregon."

He could have told the lawman other things as well; that he was twenty-four, that he had been on the move

9

for the past five years, drifting about the frontier, that he was still looking for a place — and a reason — to settle down. But he did not. He simply confined his answer to the question.

"You live around this part of Texas?"

Ricker's patience ended abruptly. "Hell, no! Was just riding through. Comanches jumped me and I lost my canteen. Spotted you and figured I'd tap you for a swallow or two of water — but if you're going to make a federal case out of it, I reckon I'll wait until I get to that settlement on ahead."

The marshal moved his shoulders slightly. Unhooking his canteen, he tossed it to Ricker. "Help yourself," he drawled.

Dan caught the container, then paused. He saw the rope then. It was knotted to the lawman's saddle and trailed back into the brush.

"Better wet a rag and squeeze a few drops into that sorrel's mouth," the marshal said. "Animal's pretty beat."

Ricker nodded. His eyes were on the second rider, now moving into the open. The rope was looped about his middle. His wrists were bound together. Showing no interest, Ricker pulled the cork from the canteen, tipped it to his lips, and drank greedily. He felt the marshal's eyes drilling into him, heard his quiet, unhurried question.

"Know this man?"

The prisoner was young, near his own age, he guessed. He was well dressed, wearing expensive, hand-tooled boots and a wide-brimmed Stetson that would have cost an ordinary cowhand three months' wages. There was a reckless cut to his features, and a salty arrogance lay uncurbed in his eyes.

Dan shook his head. "Nope. Stranger to me," he replied, and came down from the saddle.

The prisoner laughed. "He ain't from the Double Diamond, Ben. Quit fretting."

Ricker poured a quantity of water onto his bandana and squeezed it dry into the anxious sorrel's mouth. The Double Diamond — he'd heard of it. One of the big Texas ranches.

"Don't figure you'd be tellin' me so even if he was," the marshal said dryly, and slid his pistol back into its holster.

The sorrel's thirst blunted, Dan returned the canteen to the lawman. He ducked his head at the man on the black. "He somebody I'm supposed to know?"

"Name's Jack Gorman. Pa owns the Double Diamond — and most of the people in this part of Texas. Reason I was so skittish when you showed up." The lawman leaned forward and extended his hand. "I'm beggin' your pardon, Ricker. I'm Burke, marshal from Canyon City."

Dan accepted the apology and the introduction gravely.

Gorman laughed. "Don't you worry none, Grandpaw. You'll know it when Pa and my brothers show up." He paused, then added, "Or maybe you won't. Maybe you just won't ever know what hit you!"

"We'll see," Burke murmured, undisturbed. He placed his eyes on Ricker. "Expect you're wonderin' what this's all about."

Dan shrugged. "You're a lawman, and you're taking him somewhere — to Canyon City, I'd guess. Not hard to figure it out."

"And for a damn good reason," Burke said. "Jack here's a real big man. Rode into a homesteader's place one day. Nobody there but the man's wife. Jack took it in mind to have himself a time with her. Husband showed up, tried to protect her, and Jack shot him dead."

Ricker glanced at Gorman for denial or confirmation. The rancher favored him with a cool, patronizing smile.

"This all been proved?" he asked.

"In court at Canyon City. He was sentenced to hang but he broke jail — with some Double Diamond help — and lined out for Mexico. I tracked him down, and now I'm takin' him back."

"Still a far piece to Canyon City," Gorman said in a promising sort of way.

"We'll make it. And when we do, you'll swing . . ."

Again Jack laughed. "Don't go taking any bets on it."

Ricker went to the saddle. He glanced at the distant smoke plume. "Appears we're heading for the same place. All right if I ride along with you?"

Burke nodded. "Don't see why not."

They moved off through the gray saltbush and greasewood at a slow walk. After a time Ricker said, "This ranch of Gorman's — it around here close?"

"Two or three days northeast."

Dan nodded. "See why you're looking for trouble."

"Have been ever since I started," Burke said. "That's the bad thing around this part of the country. Too many men like Frank Gorman. Regular little kings. Figures he's bigger'n the law. Knows this boy of his is a no-account, that he's a killer, but it don't make no difference. Jack's his son, and that's all he thinks about."

"Counts for plenty," Gorman said quietly.

"For too much," Burke replied. "Your pa figures things are the same as they were thirty years ago when he come into this country. Don't seem to realize this here is eighteen seventy and that a man don't make his own law like he once had to."

The old lawman shifted his slight bulk and wagged his head. "Fact is, Frank Gorman won't even admit that we've got law and order. But we have, and it's every man's bounden duty to see that it's upheld no matter whose toes gets tromped on. And if we don't all start lookin' at it that way, we might just as well turn this here country back to the Comanches."

"Pa'd sure have something to say about that," Jack cut in sarcastically. "He didn't spend half his life running them off just to give it all back to them."

"Ain't sayin' he ought. Only sayin' he's got to realize there's law and order in this country now, and he's got to respect it."

"So you're hellbent on hanging me just to make him see it," Jack said, bitterness in his tone.

Burke shrugged. "You killed that homesteader. That's why you got to hang. Ain't no other reason."

"A stinking sodbuster — with a woman who was plain asking for it. Helluva poor reason —"

"What difference does it make who or what he was? You shot him down, and that's murder. Law says you've got to pay for it."

Jack Gorman's derisive manner returned. "I'll lay you odds I won't, Grandpaw." He swiveled his attention to Dan. "You can make yourself a pile of money, cowboy. Just take a few bets on whether they'll hang me or not. You can figure they won't."

Ricker felt Burke's eyes upon him and knew that Burke was waiting for some sort of a reply. He shook his head. "Man'd be a fool to bet against the law."

Gorman swore in disgust. "Reckon that proves you're a stranger around here. Nobody bucks the Gormans."

"Sounds like a real hard family," Dan said, vaguely irritated. "Just how many Gormans are there?"

Jack's eyes narrowed. He stared at Ricker speculatively. "More'n enough, mister. Something Burke's sure going to find out before we reach Canyon City."

"He's got two brothers," the lawman explained. "Both older'n him. Amos — he's Frank Gorman's first born, and just like him. Stubborn and plain mean. Then comes Yancey. Reckon he's the best of the lot, which ain't sayin' much. Jack here's the baby of the outfit. Been trouble from the day he opened his eyes. But that cuts no tallow far as Frank's concerned. Jack's a Gorman — and a Gorman can't do nothing wrong in this country."

14

Dan shrugged. It all had a familiar ring. He had run across the same situation many times on the frontier. The Frank Gormans were a plentiful breed of roughshod autocrats who brooked interference from no one, and Dan had come to understand them, if not necessarily agree with them.

They had moved into the land when it was raw and young. They had cleared it, fought and spilled their blood to hold it; and they would never surrender any of what they considered their hard-earned rights to control it — not without violence.

"Sure looks like you've cut yourself out a mighty big chore, Marshal," Ricker said, and dismissed the subject. He lifted his head, glanced to the north. The twisting spiral of smoke was near. "Be glad to reach that town. Going to treat myself to a good meal and a soft bed."

"Not a town," Jack Gorman observed. "It's Gabe Doherty's place. Freight stop. Nothing much else there."

Burke's flat eyes swung to Jack. "Friend of yours, I suppose."

"Grandpaw," the outlaw said, grinning, "everybody in this part of Texas is a friend of the Gormans. Just ain't healthy not to be."

Listening to Gorman, Dan felt his spirits sag. He had looked forward to the luxury of a bed, of a real stove-cooked supper. Now it was not to be. He shifted on his saddle wearily.

"Guess I'll just have to forget about some fancy grub and a hotel room —"

"Oh, Gabe'll put you up if you've got the price," Gorman broke in. "He rents out rooms, serves meals. Place for your horse, too."

"Sounds kind of like a one-house settlement. That all there is to it, his place?"

"A few shacks where the hired help lives. Gabe's got a freight-hauling contract. Changes teams there. Rooms are for his spare drivers, but he's always got a couple of empties. No town like you're looking for within a hundred miles of here."

"Sounds good to me," Dan said. "Been sleeping on the ground and eating my own cooking for so long, I can hardly see straight."

Burke's quiet voice broke the succeeding silence. "Ricker, you say you're headin' north — for Oregon?"

Dan nodded. "Oregon, or maybe Montana."

The lawman waited out a long minute, then said, "Could use a deputy, leastwise until I get my prisoner to Canyon City. Wouldn't be none out of your way. Interested?"

There was a thread of hope in Ben Burke's voice. Quickly Dan said, "Nope. I'm obliged for the offer, but no thanks."

"It the Gormans that's making you say that?"

"Hell, no!" Ricker flared, angered. "I've tangled with their stripe before and managed to keep my hide. I'm just not looking for a job, that's all."

Jack laughed. Burke was silent for a brief time. Finally, "Your privilege, son," he said, but there was no missing the disappointment in his tone.

16

Sympathy for the old lawman stirred Ricker. He had spoken truthfully when he declared himself unafraid of the Gormans; his refusal was based solely on his desire to remain unencumbered and responsibility-free so that he might continue his journey. He started to speak, to explain and make his position clear, but checked himself.

The ears of the sorrel had come forward suddenly. The big gelding's head snapped up, and his eyes began to show their whites. Ricker dropped his hand to the pistol on his hip. Comanches! The sorrel's fear and awareness of Indians were pronounced and unfailing. They were somewhere nearby. Listening into the hush for any telltale sound, Dan heard Burke's slow drawl again.

"Was just a thought, makin' you a deputy. Been doin' the job on my own for better'n thirty year now. Expect I can keep right on."

"Hallelujah!" Jack Gorman said in that mocking way of his. "You just keep right on dreaming, Grandpaw."

The sorrel's apprehension grew. Dan thought he heard the muted swish of a branch. He swiveled his head slowly, let his eyes search the brush. He saw nothing — but the gelding had never been wrong before.

And he was right this time. Dan's probing glance caught the dull shine of sunlight on copper skin. He drew to a halt. In a low voice, he said, "Sit easy. There's Comanches all around us."

# CHAPTER
# THREE

In the breathless hush one of the Indians cocked his rifle. The sound was ominous, abnormally loud. Dan sat motionless. The shadowy figures were apparent now, but he could not tell if it was the same party that had pursued him. He could not locate the young chief with the campaign hat.

"What do we do — just squat here and let them fill us full of lead?" Jack Gorman's strained question was a hoarse whisper loaded with fear.

"We wait," Burke replied quietly. "We'd not get ten feet if we tried to run for it. Maybe I can talk to them. Could be this here badge of mine —"

"Not yet — don't move!" Ricker flung his warning in a hurried voice as the lawman started to wheel about.

His cry came too late. A rifle cracked spitefully. Burke flinched, rocked on his saddle, and almost fell. Instantly a chorus of yells lifted. Comanches poured out of the brush in a sudden thud of hooves, to form a tight circle around the three men. The brave with the army hat was there.

Burke, his right hand clasped to his left arm, looked at Ricker grimly. "Knowed better than that. Was a dang fool stunt if ever I pulled one."

Eyes on the dark faces before him, Dan said, "You hit bad?"

"Flesh wound. Missed the bone, seems. Don't know if the beggar meant it or was just doin' some poor shootin'."

"He meant it," Ricker said, settling his attention on the arrogant brave wearing the campaign hat. "They want us alive."

"Figure to have themselves some fun, that it? Hand us over to their womenfolk to carve on."

"Doubt it. We'll be traded to the Comancheros, most likely. This bunch is after prisoners to swap for whiskey and guns."

Jack Gorman swore deeply. "The stinking bastards — they're not making no slave out of me!"

"Keep your shirt on," Dan said. "This is the same bunch I got away from this morning. Maybe we can do it again."

The chief's black eyes flared hotly. He sat erect on his pony, a fairly new rifle laid across his legs. His oily hair was pulled tight about his head and hung in braids over his chest. The sun glistened dully against the copper of his skin.

"You not get away!" he yelled in broken English. "Not any you!"

Dan Ricker realized he had erred. The Comanche had understood his words. But it was no time to show fear or surprise.

"Maybe," he said boldly. "You better think hard. This man here that you shot is the law. The government is his chief. You take us, the soldiers will come quick. They'll hang all of you."

The chief bared his teeth and spat insolently. "Faugh! I blow wind on your law! Largo not run from *gringo* soldiers. Soldiers run from Largo!"

The Comanche turned his head and barked something in quick Spanish. Two braves came off their horses and moved up to the three men.

"Want guns," Largo said. "You fight, we kill."

Ricker raised his hands slowly. "You won't kill us," he said. "Comancheros won't buy dead men."

Largo nodded. "You wise *gringo*," he said grudgingly.

Anger at the misfortune that had delivered him again into the hands of the Comanches caught up with Dan Ricker in that moment. He'd be Goddamn lucky to get out of it this time, he thought, saddled as he was with a smart-talking outlaw and a wounded marshal. Why the hell did such things have to happen to him?

The Comanches relieved them of their weapons and returned to their horses. The haul netted them three pistols for which they cared little and a rifle that meant much. All were passed out among the braves immediately.

Largo waved haughtily toward the hills to the east. "We go. Camp far."

Dan pointed to Burke. "Better let me fix his arm. Comancheros won't buy him if he's dead."

The chief scowled and rode in near to the lawman. He reached out and jerked Burke's hand away from the

20

wound. The marshal flinched. Largo stared at the bleeding wound, then motioned to Dan.

"You fix. Quick."

Ricker dropped from the saddle. Two or three braves, unaware of Largo's command, yelled and surged forward. The chief drove them back with curses in a mixture of Spanish, English, and Comanche.

Taking an old undershirt from his saddlebags, Dan ripped it into strips. He crossed to where Burke waited.

"Got no medicine," he said. "Not even some whiskey to clean the wound with. But I'll stop that bleeding."

Burke's face was gray and drawn. "Can't see as there's much point —"

"We'll get our chance," Ricker said in a low voice. "Just don't rile them. Let them think we're coming along with no trouble." He began to dress the wound, then paused as Jack Gorman's voice reached him.

"Chief, how about you and me making a bargain?"

Largo frowned, glaring at Gorman. "My pa — he's a big man. Plenty of cattle and lots of money. You let me go, I'll see you get *mucho dinero*. You understand? Then you can buy all the guns and whiskey you want."

"You're a fool to tell him that," Ricker said.

"You can let him trade you to the damn Comancheros if you want!" Jack shot back. "Me — I've got other ideas." He swung again to the Indian.

"What do you say, Chief? You ride with me to my ranch — the Double Diamond. My pa — my father will pay you plenty — silver and gold."

Largo pointed at Burke and Dan Ricker. "He pay for them, too?"

"Hell, no! You can have them."

"Now you're getting an idea of what a Gorman's like inside," Burke murmured. "Real fine people!"

"He's wasting his breath," Dan said, and resumed his chore.

"How about it, Chief? We got us a deal?"

"I blow wind on your deal!" Largo said, shrugging. "All *gringos* tell lie. No silver, only bullets for Comanches who ride with you to the place of your father."

"I give you my promise!" Gorman said in a desperate voice. "You can bring all your braves with you. I'll guarantee you that —"

"All *gringos* lie," the Indian repeated woodenly, and eased his horse over to where Ricker worked at Burke's arm. He peered at the old lawman and suddenly lashed out with his foot, driving a wicked blow into Dan's ribs.

"Enough! We ride!"

Ricker, biting back his fury, stubbornly completed the job of tying the makeshift bandage and stepped back. He centered his attention on Burke, fighting off the temptation to spin, to seize the Comanche and drag him off his horse.

"Best I can do. Maybe when we get to their camp I can find something —"

"We go!" Largo shouted. "Lie-teller *gringo*, we go!"

He aimed a second kick at the tall man's body, but Ricker jerked away, still battling the anger that swelled through him. Ignoring the circle of dark, sweaty faces grinning down at him, he swung onto the sorrel.

"Go!" Largo said, pointing to the hills. "Go fast!"

They moved out of the swale, the three men riding abreast, with the Comanches ranging about them in a loose half circle. When they reached the top of the rise and were on a flat, Largo pulled out in front. As chief, it was befitting he lead the successful party into camp.

They continued to bear eastward for a long line of brush-covered hills and buttes. Dan Ricker had lapsed into hot, simmering resentment and exasperation at the twist matters had taken for him, but Burke, apparently pleased at one thing, at least, looked slyly at his prisoner and chuckled.

"One time the Gorman name sure didn't cut no mustard, eh, Jack?"

"This ain't over," the outlaw snapped. "I'll talk that redskin son of a bitch into a deal yet. You'll see."

He would never succeed, Dan knew. The Comanches placed no trust in any white man. They had been fooled too often. With the Comancheros — usually Mexicans and sometimes renegade Americans — he might have a chance. They had been known to bargain, to accept ransom when conditions warranted. But that was something Jack Gorman could find out for himself.

Near the middle of the afternoon the sorrel began to tire, but Ricker knew it would be useless to complain to Largo. Comanches thought little of horseflesh, gave their animals no consideration of any sort. If feed and water were available, their mounts ate and drank; if not, they suffered. Rest was a thing unheard-of. Horses were too easily stolen to worry over.

He doubted they were far from the camp, anyway. Earlier he had caught the smell of greasewood smoke in the air, and since they were in country inhabited solely by Indians, it could mean only that the rest of Largo's band was near. Dan did not wonder at what lay ahead for him and the two men at his side, once they were there; he knew exactly. They would be traded to the Comancheros.

The interests of the ruthless traders were varied. They dealt in stolen horses and cattle, merchandise removed from captured freight wagons, household goods, and such items procured by raiding immigrant trains. Most particularly, however, they sought women and girls for the brothels and army camps, and men for working the mines below the border. Once there, escape was admittedly impossible, and that truth now occupied Dan Ricker's thought processes. Wiping at the sweat gathered on his brow, he tried to concentrate on a means for escape before the Indians could consummate a deal with the Comancheros.

It would be one hell of a job. Burke was wounded, and he could expect little if any help from Jack Gorman. They had no weapons and could figure on being under close guard at all times. How long they would remain captives of the Indians was anybody's guess; until the Comancheros showed up, that was certain — and that could be days, even weeks. Their one hope lay there, Ricker concluded; the longer they were held prisoner, the better their chances of escape.

Dan became aware that Largo had halted. The chief was looking off to his right, to an area hidden from Ricker and the others by a tall screen of hackberry and thick brush. Suddenly the Comanche cupped his hands to his mouth and yelled.

Immediately an answering cry came from beyond the dense growth. The braves behind the captives added their shouts to that of Largo, and the entire party moved on. They circled the thicket and broke out into a fair-sized hollow where a scatter of trees clustered about a spring. Beyond that Dan saw the Comanche camp — two dozen or more crude shelters, a corral of horses, numerous dogs, and thirty or forty more Indian men, women, and children.

And Dan Ricker saw something else. In a fenced enclosure somewhat apart from the camp, stood a canvas-covered wagon. Beside it was a white woman — actually a girl barely out of her teens. She watched them ride in, and even from the distance Dan Ricker could see the lift of hope in her expression.

Angry frustration swept through Ricker. As if things weren't bad enough — now he had a woman on his hands to look out for.

# CHAPTER
# FOUR

Largo rode into camp proud and arrogant. At once the dogs set up a loud clamor, and the entire band of Comanches swarmed into the cleared area around which the shelters had been erected, shouting questions, pawing at the prisoners, and hurling insults. One small boy seized a stone and hurled it at Jack Gorman, hitting him on the leg.

Dan Ricker sat in stony silence on the sorrel. He could understand only a small amount of what was being said, now and then picking up a few words of the Spanish. Along with some cattle and another *gringo* captive — apparently the girl — they were to be traded to the Comancheros, as he had suspected. The renegades were expected soon.

His glory established satisfactorily, Largo gave a harsh command. A half dozen braves closed in about Ricker and the other two Americans, drove off the squaws and children with shouts and blows, and led the captives to the enclosure.

The three men were dragged from their saddles and shoved roughly through the makeshift gate. Burke, weakened by his wound, went full length into the dust. Ricker and Gorman managed to keep their feet.

With the sound of Jack's steady cursing in his ears, Dan watched the Indians lead their horses off to a second corral at the rear of the village where other horses were being penned. There was water for the animals, he saw, if not much in the way of grass. But he was more interested at that moment in where the animals would be; without a horse, escape was utterly impossible.

He turned then to Burke and helped him to rise. In that same moment he became aware of the other prisoner. She had moved up from the wagon and now stood before him. She was, as he had guessed, around nineteen or perhaps twenty. Despite her ragged, filthy clothing she was pretty, with a wealth of sunflower-colored hair and steady brown eyes that met his squarely.

"I'm — I'm Marfa Talbot," she began in a firm voice. "I'm glad you —"

Her voice broke suddenly. She lowered her head as her quiet self-control vanished and her shoulders began to move convulsively. Jack Gorman stepped in hurriedly and took her in his arms. She stiffened and regained her composure.

"I'm glad . . . you're here . . ."

"We're prisoners — same as you," Ricker snapped, impatient with himself, with the hopelessness of the situation, and with Marfa Talbot's tears.

"I know. But alone . . . it's been so terrible . . ."

"How long you been here?" Burke asked in a kindly voice.

"A week — maybe a little over. They killed my father when they stopped our wagon. Brought us here. Mama died three days ago. I buried her myself . . . over there."

She motioned indefinitely toward the back of the enclosure. Abruptly she pulled away from Gorman. Her eyes were bright, her features strained.

"What will they do to us — kill us, too?"

"Doubt it," Ricker said. "We're worth plenty to them alive."

Marfa frowned. "Why? What would they want —"

Ricker turned away, electing to tell her no more. Having the girl to look out for was bad enough without causing her to go all to pieces when she learned what lay in store for her should any attempt to escape fail. But Jack had other ideas.

"Don't let him bother you, Marfa," he said quietly. "He's riled because of the fix we're in — and you being here makes it worse. The Indians figure to sell us to the Comancheros. That's why they won't hurt us none."

"Comancheros? Who are they?"

"Traders. Do business with the Indians. Buy the stuff they've stolen, resell it."

"But how — where do we come in?"

"They'll sell us, too. In Mexico. Men end up in the silver and gold mines. Women — well, the women —"

"Drop it, Jack," Ricker cut in sharply. "No use making it worse."

Marfa Talbot's face was stiff. "I understand," she said quietly. Again her glance met that of Ricker. "And don't worry about me. I won't be any problem to you. Just let

28

me go with you if you're planning to escape. I promise I won't hold you back . . ."

Ricker shrugged and again turned away to study the irregular stockade-like fence that surrounded the yard.

Burke said, "Don't worry, Miss. We'll get you out of here. Just you leave it to us."

Dan swore under his breath. He wished he could be as optimistic as the old lawman; if Burke thought it was going to be easy to get out he was a plain damn fool.

The fence was not high, and in many places rabbit-brush, tumbleweeds, and other rank growth all but hid it. It was constructed of poles and bits of wire and rope, all firmly bound together. Dan wheeled back to the girl. She was talking with Burke. Jack Gorman had moved over to the fence where several Comanche braves loitered. Evidently he was trying to interest them in ransom again.

"They keep guards posted around here all the time?" Ricker asked.

"Only at night," Marfa replied. "Usually one on each side. They don't bother about it in the daytime. Guess they knew I couldn't get far."

"Don't see how we can either," Burke said, changing his tune. "We got no guns — or horses. How you figure we can get around that?"

Ricker idly watched Jack Gorman turn away from the Comanches at the fence, to walk slowly and dejectedly back toward the wagon. Apparently his offer had fallen on deaf ears for the second time.

"Don't know yet," Dan said, "but we've got to try — tonight, if possible. They're looking for the Comancheros to show up any minute."

He glanced at Marfa Talbot, gauging her reaction. She accepted the information without flinching. After a moment she said, "Is there anything I can do to help?"

"The guards," Dan said. "Where do they usually stand?"

"One on each side. About the middle of the fence."

"There only one gate?"

She nodded. On beyond her Ricker could see the horse corral. The sorrel was moving about among the smaller Indian ponies searching for grass. The saddle and bridle had not been removed. Looking further, he located Burke's buckskin and Gorman's black. They, too, still carried their gear.

Likely they would become more merchandise for trading to the Comancheros. The Indians would not want the saddles and bridles, scorning them as useless items that slowed the pace of a running horse. And while the three animals might be far better than any of their own starved ponies, they would recognize their bartering value and consider it more profitable to hand them over to the renegades in trade.

It would not be hard to reach the corral, Dan saw, fixing the lay of the land in his mind. The problem would be getting over the fence and out of the enclosure without being seen. Ricker's thoughts came to a full stop. Why not under the fence? He glanced to Marfa Talbot.

30

"There a spade or a shovel — something we can dig with in your wagon?"

She thought for a moment, then said, "Yes. I remember we had to dig ourselves out of the mud once —"

"You figure to tunnel under the fence — that it?" Burke asked, getting the idea quick.

Dan nodded. Gorman shrugged. "Play hell doing that with guards around. Ground's hard as nails. They'll hear you sure."

"Not if we get rid of the guard first," Dan replied. "You're sure that shovel's still in your wagon?" he added, facing Marfa.

"I'm sure," she answered, "but — I just happened to remember — there's already a hole under the fence. I've seen the dogs come through it."

"Where?" Ricker demanded, his hopes rising swiftly. "Don't point, just tell me."

"There in that corner where that forked post is."

"I see it," Dan said. It was in the side of the fence opposite that which faced the horse corral. Making use of it would call for a long doubling back once they were outside, but it was a good bet — likely their only one.

"Any idea how much of a hole it is?"

"No, but all the dogs come through it."

"Seen some pretty fair-sized ones out there," Burke volunteered.

Dan nodded. "It'll be big enough. We'll dig it out a bit if we have to."

He centered his attention again on the fence and began to trace a path from the hole along the north side of the enclosure to where the horses were penned. There was little cover to shield their movements from the camp. It would be impossible during the daylight hours, but at night . . .

The plan began to grow and take shape. He pivoted to the wagon. He could see the blankets used as bedding and the canvas upon which they were spread, piled in the back.

Ben Burke's voice broke into his thoughts. "Got somethin' figured out?"

"Maybe. It'll be a long shot, but it could work if —"

His words checked abruptly. The high, shrill squeal of wheels turning on ungreased axles grated in his ears.

"What the devil is that!" the lawman exclaimed, wheeling about. "Never heard such a racket!"

Ricker's face was solemn as he listened to the nerve-shattering screech. "*Carretas*," he said finally. "Two-wheeled wagons — the kind the Comancheros do their hauling in. Means they're here."

# CHAPTER
# FIVE

There were ten horsemen and one *carreta* in the party. They halted in the center of the camp. Immediately squaws, braves, and children surged toward it, gathered around, and began to examine its contents excitedly. Dan could see several small whiskey kegs in the cargo, but he was too far away to determine just what else had been brought by the Comancheros.

Largo stood a little apart, austere and cool, ignoring the activity with the disdain befitting a chief. The leader of the renegades, a squat, blocky man in the remnants of an army uniform and a wide-brimmed, silver-trimmed Mexican *sombrero*, dismounted and approached the Comanche. He raised his hand and held it palm outward in the customary salutation. Largo responded stiffly. The remaining Comancheros, a collection of rough, filthy hardcases, stayed on their saddles all the while, eyeing the chattering Comanches warily.

Grim, Dan Ricker watched in silence.

Burke moved in beside him. "You got somethin' figured, we'd better be gettin' at it," he murmured.

"Nothing we can do until dark," Ricker replied. "If those Comancheros take a notion to get their trading done fast and ride on tonight, we're up against it for sure."

"Indians like palaverin'," the lawman said. "Could last till mornin'."

Ricker reached for his cigarette makings. At that moment Largo and the leader of the renegades wheeled and headed for the enclosure. A dozen braves and the mounted Comancheros followed at a short distance.

"Coming to look us over," Dan said. He glanced at the lawman. "Turn sideways. Don't let them see that bad arm of yours."

Burke shifted his position, placing his good shoulder to the fence. "Maybe I ought to let the bugger see it. Might figure I wasn't no bargain."

Ricker shrugged impatiently. "Go ahead. Be a quick way to end up in the hands of the squaws."

The marshal grinned wryly. "No thanks. 'Druther take my chances with the Comancheros."

Largo and the renegade chief stopped at the line of posts. The Indian waved his hand toward the captives.

"Young woman. Yellow hair. Strong men. All fine shape."

The Comanchero touched each of the prisoners with sharp, critical eyes. He brought his gaze to a halt on Marfa. He looked the girl up and down, his mouth slowly cracking into a wide grin.

"Now, you sure did, Largo! You done yourself right proud." He continued to rake Marfa with his hard, glittering stare. "The old man ain't much, but the others will do — especially that yaller-haired gal. You been keepin' your braves away from her?"

"Braves no touch!" the Comanche chief declared haughtily. "I, Largo, say them not to. My word strong."

"Sure, I know that," the Comanchero said. "Just wanted to find out —"

"Largo every time honest with friend Chino. No tell him lies."

Ricker cast a side glance at Marfa. She stood erect, returned Chino's bold appraisal defiantly with level eyes. If she felt fear she did not reveal it. A grudging respect stirred within Dan Ricker.

"That's right," the Comanchero agreed. "And I always treat my Comanche friends good. Now, let's see them steers and horses."

Largo did not stir. "How much for them?" he demanded in his guttural voice, pointing at the captives. "Worth plenty. Soldiers pay much for girl."

Chino clawed at the black stubble covering his chin. Sweat lay in patches on his cheekbones and forehead, glistening in the lowering sunlight. "Well, now I ain't got down to figurin' exact yet, Chief, but it'll be fair. I ain't never cheated you yet, have I?"

Largo nodded. "Chino my friend. But how much you pay? Girl with yellow hair worth much. Want plenty whiskey, many guns and bullets for her."

"She's worth plenty — long as she ain't been touched . . ."

"Largo tell you no. Largo no lie!"

"I'm takin' your word for it, but I got to see them steers and horses afore we do any bargainin'. Anyway, we ought to be doin' our yammerin' over a barrel of red-eye, not standin' out here. Now, where you got them animals?"

Largo considered for a moment, then nodded. It was plain he was not pleased to have the Comancheros in his camp, yet realized he must countenance them if he were to accomplish his purpose.

"We go," he said abruptly, and barked an order to one of his braves.

The Comanche spun at once and trotted to where several ponies stood. Others turned to follow, and in a few moments all returned, mounted and leading a horse for their chief. Chino swung onto his own mount, and the party rode off eastward, heading into a narrow draw.

Dan glanced at the sun. The dickering, once whiskey began to flow, could take hours — at least he hoped it would. But it was best not to depend on it.

"Reckon we ain't got much time left," Burke said quietly. "They're gettin' right down to business."

Ricker nodded and again gauged the sun. Gorman shrugged. "Still figure I can make a deal with them, buy our way out of this."

Burke came about in surprise. "All of us?"

"All of us — if I can come to terms with you."

"Meanin' what?"

"If I can deal with Chino or the Indian to let us go — you forget about me and Canyon City."

The lawman was silent for a long time. Finally he shook his head. "Can't do that."

"Not even if it means they turn us loose? Hell, think about the girl, Burke. Think what they've got waiting for her. Rest of us, too."

"You can't buy your way out of this," Dan cut in. "Might as well forget it."

"You'd be surprised what a handful of gold can do for a man," Gorman insisted.

"I've seen what it can do," Dan replied. "Right now it counts for nothing. Once Chino gets his hands on us we won't get a chance to look up until we're in Mexico. Maybe — just maybe — after we're there you might save your own neck by bribing a guard or two. But it will be too late for anything else."

Gorman shrugged. "Don't see it that way — and I'm willing to try now." He turned to Burke. "Reckon it's up to you, Marshal. Forget me and the hangman's rope, and I'll —"

"Ricker's right," Burke said. "I'll string along with him because he's talkin' sense." The lawman glanced to Dan. "Anythin' we ought to be doin' about gettin' ready?"

"We make our move after it's dark. We try something before that, we'll stir up their suspicions."

"What've you got in mind?"

Dan pointed to the wagon. "Indians've got used to seeing the girl sleeping there. We'll make another bed close by for ourselves. Time comes, we'll turn in too, only we won't stay put long. We'll rig some dummies out of quilts and clothing and the like, stuff them under the blankets."

"Make them think we're still there," Burke said.

"What good will all that do?" Jack demanded. "You heard her say there was guards outside the fence."

"Long as they stay outside, they're no problem. Seems all they do is glance this way now and then. And if they see us under the blankets — or think they do — they won't come any closer."

"So they see us. Then what? How'll that help us?"

"Burke and I will take care of the two guards along the fence, the one that'll be standing near the hole, and the other along the side of the fence that leads to the horse corral. When they're out of the way, we'll crawl under."

"Still two other guards — and the braves in camp. One of them's bound to miss the two you aim to kill."

"When we're finished with them they'll still be there in full sight," Ricker said quietly.

"Tie 'em to one of the posts, that it?" Burke said. "Ought to work fine. We can grab their guns, too."

"Sounds too easy," Gorman said skeptically. "What am I going to be doing all that time?"

"You and the girl stay under the blankets, make things look real as possible. When we've got the guards out of the way, we'll signal. You two get down flat, crawl to the hole. We'll be waiting there for you."

"One thing," Burke said thoughtfully. "Bein' outside ain't gettin' away. What do we do then?"

"Crawl some more — on our bellies all the way to the corral."

"Could be a guard with them horses."

"Maybe, but I doubt it. We'll take no chances, and move in easy. Once we've got horses we're in good shape. And if Chino and Largo get to wrangling, we can be a long way from here before they find out we're gone."

"Hell of a lot of ifs in this," Gorman said sourly.

"Better than gettin' hauled off to Mexico," Burke shot back. "Expect the girl will agree to that."

Marfa nodded. "I'm ready to try anything."

Dan studied her. "I hope so," he said. "But it's going to be close — touch-and-go every second. Hope you can stand up to it — not go to pieces."

Marfa stiffened. Anger flashed in her eyes. "You've doubted me from the moment you rode in, and you've made it clear you've got no use for me — maybe not for any woman."

"There's nothing personal —" Dan began, but she cut him short.

"I'm not any happier about being here than you are — and I want to get away just as bad. So don't worry about me not holding up my end of the —"

A shout went up from the Comanche camp. Dan and the others turned their attention to that point. Largo and the Comanchero leader were coming back after viewing the stolen cattle. Now the bargaining would begin. While they watched, two of the renegades lifted a keg off the cart and rolled it to the center of the clearing. Tipping it on end, the taller of the pair drove his boot heel through the head. Liquor splashed onto the ground as the wood splintered.

More yells went up, and the Comanches — men, women, and children — rushed in eagerly, each carrying a cup, a gourd, an empty bottle, or a pan with which to help themselves. The Comancheros, finally off their saddles, joined in. Someone threw more fuel on the fire, and the flames leaped upward, lighting the clearing. The shouting increased, interspersed with laughter and the barking of dogs.

Ricker glanced to the west. The sun was just setting. He turned to the others. "Let's start getting ready. We've got about an hour."

# CHAPTER
# SIX

By the time night had set in to cover the brushy hills and deep arroyos with black shadows, the Comanche camp was a bedlam of howling, dancing savages. A second keg of whiskey had been broached, and there was not one man, woman, or child old enough to swallow who was not drunk.

Dan Ricker, with Burke at his side, crouched in the solid darkness beneath the Talbot wagon. At an opportune moment they had crawled from under their blankets, substituting wads of clothing supplied by Marfa in suitable mounds to simulate their own shapes. The girl still remained on her pallet under the tarp, as did Jack Gorman on his.

There were four braves spaced along the fence as Marfa had said there would be. All had partaken generously of the whiskey keg's contents before assuming their positions, and they were in only little better condition than Largo and the others cavorting around the blazing fire.

They were still in fair control of their faculties, however; Dan had determined this by tossing a small rock beyond them into the brush. Both had reacted instantly, if unsteadily.

It would be no easy task to slip up on them, and because of that Ricker found himself faced with a decision. He mulled it about in his mind for several minutes while they waited, and when at last he knew that longer delay would be dangerous, he turned to Burke.

"Marshal, that arm of yours is giving you trouble. I've been watching you favor it. We don't want anything to trip us up, so I think we'd better figure on Jack taking care of that guard and you staying with the girl."

Gorman drew himself to an elbow. "Smartest thing you've said yet, Ricker. The old man will get us caught sure, using that bum arm."

Burke stared down at his prisoner for a moment. "That what you're thinkin' — or you thinkin' it'll mean you'll get your hands on a gun — and maybe make a run for it on your own?"

"Thought of that," Ricker said before Gorman could reply. "I'll be responsible for him — see to it that he doesn't get away. Main thing is we've got to get out of here."

Burke nodded. "It's all right with me, only I'm warnin' you, Jack, if you cross us up and slip out of my hands, it ain't done with! I'll just start all over again huntin' you down. And I'll find you. Makes no difference where you go."

Gorman said, "Sure . . . sure," and crawled from under the tarp. Burke worked himself back into the blankets.

Ricker picked up a short length of rope he had scrounged from the Talbots' meager possessions and tossed it to Gorman. He had another of similar size tucked inside his shirt front.

"Got to do this fast and quiet. You take the Indian across from us. I'll jump the one on the right. Crawl all the way. And when you get that rope around his neck, jerk it tight. Don't let him yell."

"I know," Jack mumbled impatiently.

Dan glanced at Burke. He would have preferred trusting the chore to the lawman, but the man's wound would slow him, possibly allow a moment in which the Comanche he was assigned to remove could sing out and warn the others. And they could afford no mistakes.

"You know the signal," he said then to the older man. "When I whistle twice, bring the girl. Stay low."

The lawman said, "We'll be waitin'."

Ricker cast a final look at the camp. A dozen or so braves, brandishing rifles evidently turned over to them by the Comancheros, were performing a wild dance around the fire, to the accompaniment of shouts and the sullen thump of improvised drums. Both Largo and Chino were hunched before one of the shelters watching.

"When you're done," Dan said to Gorman, "meet me at the corner where the hole is."

He did not turn to see if the man heard; he simply held his eyes on the camp; he must be certain none of the braves decided unexpectedly to head for the enclosure. All appeared to be preoccupied with the noisy activities.

"Now," Ricker murmured, and dropping flat on the warm, sandy ground, he crawled off into the darkness.

Dan lost sight of Gorman immediately when the man dropped down into a shallow gully. He pulled himself silently toward the silhouette of the Comanche leaning against the fence twenty yards or so away. He had been unable to tell from the wagon if the brave faced him or was turned. He covered half the distance, then looked. The Indian was slumped against a post, chin sunk into his chest. Ricker hoped Jack Gorman's luck was equally good.

He continued, working his way slowly, carefully. The ground was dry, baked hard by the summer sun, and it was not too difficult to move. He had to be doubly cautious with the scrawny brush and weeds, however; the slightest contact set up a rattle of brittle leaves and branches.

He paused again and lifted his head. The Comanche was no more than ten feet distant. Moonlight glinted off the rifle resting against his leg. He was either asleep or in a drunken stupor — Dan had no idea which. It did not matter. Ricker was simply grateful for his good fortune. He pulled himself forward another arm's length and halted abruptly.

A yell had gone up — but it was near. It had come from somewhere between the camp and the enclosure. Fear caught at Ricker's throat. He flattened out, twisted around, glanced toward the fire. Three braves, barely able to stay on their feet, were headed for the fence. Ricker watched them approach, hoping fervently that Jack Gorman had also seen them.

The Indians staggered up to the guard standing along the fence that faced the camp. They were shouting and laughing. Each had a bottle of whiskey in his hand. They halted. One offered his container of liquor to the sentry. The Comanche seized it, held it to his mouth, and drank greedily. The guard thrust the empty bottle at its owner, lurched to one side, and made a grab for a bottle belonging to one of the other Comanches.

Instantly a scuffle broke out. The two men wrestled back and forth. The bottle dropped, shattering against a rock. A new chorus of yells went up, and the pair pulled apart. There were a few moments of loud, angry conversation, and then the three braves reeled back toward the camp.

Relief coursed through Dan Ricker. He lay quiet for a time, breathing deeper, listening to the curses hurled by the sentry at his departing friends. Finally that ceased, and Dan rolled to his stomach. He looked ahead. The guard, directly in front of him, had been aroused by the noisy altercation. He now faced the fire.

Dan hung motionless, afraid to make the slightest move, almost fearing to breathe. The Indian shouted something to the man on the opposite side of the enclosure, a guttural, derisive-sounding word that had no meaning for Ricker. And then he pivoted slowly and placed his shoulders against the post.

Once more, relief poured through Ricker. He brushed at the sweat clouding his eyes, swallowed, tried to ease the tenseness of his muscles. While he watched, the Comanche settled down and relaxed. Dan waited out five more minutes, then began to inch forward again. Unwilling to raise his head at that point, he fastened his gaze on the base of the post; that would be his goal.

He gained a position where he could reach out and touch the dry, shaggy bark. He could hear the Comanche's breathing — deep rasps, almost snores. Cautiously, Ricker lifted himself. The Indian was an arm's length away. Ricker twisted slowly and glanced at the camp, hopeful of no more visitors. No one was coming.

Silently he pulled his legs beneath his body. He took the short length of rope and crossed it, shaping a loop but avoiding a knot. He wished only to have the tough strands pulling against each other; a knot would be slow and would actually reduce the sudden pressure he desired. He glanced to the adjacent fence. He could not see Gorman, and the guard still leaned against a post.

Apprehension gripped Ricker. Jack should have completed his job by that moment. He had a lesser distance to cover than Ricker. What was holding him back? Dan shook his head and put aside the question. He could not worry about Gorman; it was up to the man to carry his part of the scheme.

Ricker drew himself to a crouch. With the rope ready in his hands, he bent over the top of the fence. Silently, carefully, he lowered the loop until it was around the Comanche's neck. Putting all his strength into it, he jerked the rope taut.

A gasp exploded from the brave's lips. He surged to his feet. The loop checked him. He fell back against the post, clawing frantically at the throttling cord about his throat. His rifle slid to the ground as he began to stiffen. Ricker maintained his relentless pulling at the ends of the rope. Finally the Comanche wilted and sagged into a limp shape. Pausing long enough to glance toward the camp again, assuring himself that he had not been noticed, Dan hunched over, dragged the Indian to an upright position, and bound him to the post.

He snatched up the fallen rifle. His hands searched the Comanche's body for other weapons. He found only a dozen or so extra cartridges for the gun, tied in a small square of ragged cloth. Thrusting them into his pocket, he sank to his knees and crawled hurriedly for the corner where Marfa had said there was a hole.

He reached it at almost the same moment as did Jack Gorman. He studied the outlaw's sweat-plastered face briefly. "Any trouble?"

The wildness of the man boiled over in his voice. When he spoke the sheer thrill of the last few minutes shone through his words. "None. Was a cinch. That red son of a bitch was dead before he knew it."

Ricker turned and checked the hole. It would be large enough to permit their crawling under the fence. He looked then to the camp. There was no lessening of the riotous dancing and carousing. Lifting his head, Dan whistled twice into the warm darkness. Immediately he heard Burke's reply. They would be coming.

Dan moved to the corner of the fence and quietly pulled aside the weeds blown in by the winds. He

47

motioned to Gorman. "We'll crawl through now. Save time."

He ducked into the opening. His hips dragged against the sides, but he squirmed free. Keeping low in the bushes and rocks, he waited for Gorman.

Jack worked himself under the fence, puffing at the unusual exertion. He drew up close to Ricker and pointed toward the corral. "Might be smart for me to get the horses, have them ready."

Ricker gave that no consideration. Had it been someone other than Jack Gorman he might have agreed, but he placed no trust in the man, and he had given his assurance to Ben Burke.

"No. We keep together."

Gorman muttered under his breath and settled back. Dan touched the rifle he held. "That all the guard had?"

"Was all. Not even a knife on him."

"How about extra cartridges?"

"Didn't find none."

That was a blow. They would have little ammunition with which to fight if their escape were discovered and pursuit followed. Their only hope now lay in getting away safely without being forced to shoot it out.

"Ricker?" It was Burke's hoarse whisper.

Dan said, "Come on through. Keep down."

Marfa Talbot appeared first, her face a pale, strained oval in the half darkness. Burke followed, grunting and muttering at his injured arm. Breathing heavily, he drew up beside Dan.

"We've done it so far. Now what?"

48

"We go back along the fence to the corral. Stay close — and out of sight." He paused and glanced at Marfa. "It's a long two hundred yards. Don't think we'll run into any more guards unless it's the one on that side of the fence. If we do, flatten out and be quiet. I'll take care of him."

Dan pulled away from the brush, then hesitated when he heard Burke's voice. "I'll be takin' that rifle, Jack."

Gorman snorted. "You will like hell. I'm hanging on to it."

Ricker flung a look toward the Indian camp. There was no time to waste arguing. He motioned impatiently to Gorman. "Give it to him. You know the deal."

Gorman stalled for several moments, inclined to refuse. He thought better of it and passed the weapon to Burke.

"We get jumped, you damn well better be able to use it!"

"I'm just hopin' I won't have to use it on you," the lawman replied quietly.

Ricker moved off at once. There was a slight ridge a pace or two north of the fence, something he had not noticed earlier. It offered protection, and he saw that they could walk at a crouch, rather than crawl on their hands and knees. And they could travel faster. He looked over his shoulder. Behind him was Marfa. She was followed by Gorman. Burke brought up the rear.

Ricker led them to the ridge, and they hurried on with the racket of the camp loud in their ears. They came abreast of the brave he had suspended from the post. The unexpected appearance of the Comanche brought an involuntary gasp from the girl, but she said nothing.

They reached the corner of the enclosure. The horses, dozing in their crude corral, were only a short distance ahead. Ricker halted and threw his gaze along the east line of the irregular fence. The guard, hunched beside a large rock, was a dark shadow, midway down. Dan watched the Comanche for a brief time. The man was not moving, was either asleep or drunk, as had been the other sentry. But their route to the corral crossed directly in front of him, and Ricker would take no chances.

"Wait here," he whispered. "Listen for my whistle."

He crawled over the fence, grateful for the dark bulk of the Talbots' wagon looming up between him and the campfire. He wormed his way to where the guard sat, continued on until he was a few paces beyond, and again climbed the fence. He had no rope this time; he must rely on other means to silence the man.

With soft, deliberate steps, he doubled back, holding his rifle overhead as a club. He reached the Comanche, raised the gun higher, and started it downward in a swift, crushing blow.

In that fragment of time the Indian, alerted by some inner force, opened his eyes. He saw Ricker standing over him, saw the oncoming rifle barrel streaking for his head. A fearful yell broke from his lips — and died abruptly in a groan as Ricker's weapon smashed his skull.

But the damage was done.

50

Someone — certainly the other sentry — would have heard the man's scream. Wasting no time, Dan rushed across the open ground for the corral. Halfway there he sent a low whistled summons to Burke and the others. From the tail of his eye he saw them move out of the shadows at the corner of the fence and hurry to meet him.

Alarm swept through him. From the far side of the enclosure, he heard the sound of men running, of questions being yelled into the night.

# CHAPTER
# SEVEN

Ricker gained the corral a stride ahead of the others. There was no time to look for a gate, and he squeezed between the horizontally laid poles with Marfa Talbot at his heels. He halted in the center of the yard and swung his glance about in search of the sorrel. The gelding was in a far corner. Nearby were Gorman's black and the lawman's buckskin.

"Other side — quick!" he said in a sharp tone, and started through the milling horses.

"Got to pick a mount for the lady," Burke said. "And these Indian ponies ain't got no saddle. Reckon she'd better use mine."

"No," Ricker said. "With that bad arm be better for you to keep your buckskin. I'll use one of their ponies."

He reached the sorrel, seized the reins, and wheeled him around. Marfa was moving toward one of the Indian horses.

"Here," he said, "you're taking my sorrel."

She paused and looked back at him. "Never mind. I can ride bareback."

Anger rushed through Dan Ricker. He threw a glance toward the camp, hurried to her. "Goddammit

— I said to take my horse!" he snapped, and thrust the reins into her hands.

He strode on past her and grabbed the hackamore of the first Indian pony he saw. "Don't mount," he called, leading the animal toward the fence. "We'll walk for a ways. They'll see us if we ride."

Throwing aside the two ropes that served to close the corral, Ricker continued into the brush. He was purposely leaving the corral open in hopes that the remaining horses would get out and scatter. Such would not halt pursuit, he knew. The Comancheros had their mounts picketed on the far side of the camp. There would be Indian ponies with them too.

He glanced over his shoulder as the others trailed him into the first draw. A low hill blocked his view of the camp, but the bright flare of the fires in the night marked its location. Considerable racket still lifted from that point, and he guessed that no alarm had yet been given at the enclosure. It was a temporary respite; the braves who had gone to investigate the yell would soon discover their slain brother — and then the hunt would begin.

They reached the end of the arroyo. Ricker halted. "Safe to mount up now," he said, "but take it slow — leastwise, for a bit farther. Less noise we make the better."

He dropped back a few paces, intending to assist Marfa onto the sorrel, but Jack Gorman was a step ahead of him. Dan wheeled abruptly and vaulted onto his own pony.

"Let the girl lead off," he said, facing Burke. "Want her out —"

"Stop calling me *the girl!*" Marfa broke in angrily. She looked small but very determined on the big gelding. "My name is Marfa Talbot."

"All right, Marfa Talbot," Ricker said icily. "Get up ahead and stay there. Burke'll tell you which direction to take."

Her chances for escape would be better with Burke, Gorman, and himself in between her and any pursuing Comanches, Dan reasoned, but he did not bother to explain. A sound to their left brought him around. A half dozen of the horses had followed them out of the corral. He studied them briefly, then motioned to Burke.

"Move on around the hill and wait for me."

The lawman frowned. "Now what're you aimin' to do?"

Ricker indicated the straying ponies. "Run them down that draw to the south. Might throw the Comanches off our trail right at the start."

Burke grinned appreciatively. "Make 'em think we went that way, eh? Dang smart idea. We'll meet you up there by that butte."

Dan swung in behind the loose ponies and hazed them off to the side. Pushing them to a trot, he drove them for a good two hundred yards before he cut away and doubled back to rejoin his party. If there had been time he would have paused to wipe out his tracks, but he felt he was pressing his luck as it was.

He was still puzzled by the failure of the Indians to discover their escape. Mulling it over, the only explanation he was finally able to come up with was that the braves attracted by the yell of the guard were so liquor-befuddled themselves that they were having trouble moving about.

"Where we makin' for?" Burke asked when they were once again all together and moving along the base of the bluff.

"Doherty's place," Dan replied. "Seems it's the closest thing to a settlement around here."

He broke the horses into a lope when they reached the end of the cliffs, certain they would not be heard at that distance. There still had been no outcry or indication that they had been missed, and when they were at last moving along the edge of the foothills, he began to feel better about it all.

Luck had been with them. It was conceivable that their disappearance would not be noticed until daylight — but he wouldn't ask, or dare hope, for that. Two or three hours — that was all they needed. With such a lead he would not have to worry about the Comancheros and Largo's braves overtaking them.

They rode on through the night, pausing only briefly now and then to rest the horses. Near dawn Ricker called a halt below the rim of a long, sandy ridge, intending to extend the break for at least an hour. There was little water in the canteens, not enough for their mounts, but sufficient to allow each traveler a swallow. All were feeling hunger, but the small supply of food Dan and Burke had had in their saddlebags had been exhausted the previous day. And the Comanches had never got around to feeding them. But that discomfort would end soon; there would be plenty to eat at Doherty's.

"How far you reckon we are from that freight stop?" Burke asked as they strolled about on the slope, easing their worn muscles.

Ricker stared off toward the north. The long fingers of daylight were shooting up into the sky from the east, and the gray was fast disappearing.

"Ought to reach there by noon, unless I'm off my bearings," he said. "The girl," he added. "Is she holding out all right?"

"Doin' fine," Burke replied. "Reckon they don't come much better'n her."

"Guess not," Dan said idly.

"You and her ought to get together. Ain't no sense in the two of you actin' like a couple of strange cats to each other. Why don't you give her half a chance?"

"We're not out of this yet," Ricker said stiffly. He ducked his head at Gorman and Marfa sitting on a sand ledge a dozen yards away conversing quietly. "Looks like Jack's taking care of her, anyway."

"Been tryin' to make time with her ever since we left that Indian camp — but he ain't gettin' nowhere. Not that it'd do him any good if he did — he's still got a rope waitin' for him."

The lawman paused, his eyes on Marfa. "She sure is a pretty little thing. Them Comancheros are going to be powerful mad when they find out we've got away. Seein' as how they've done paid that Largo for her —

and us — my guess is they'll do a lot of lookin' before they give up."

"*If* they give up," Dan murmured, turning away.

He began a slow, swinging search of the horizon, beginning with the west and moving on to the south. When he reached the rim to the southeast, he came to abrupt attention. Far beyond the short, bubble-like hills, he saw a faint haze. It moved slowly toward them, a thin, compact boil of yellow. He studied it intently. It was too small, too concentrated, for one of the usual sandstorms, too near earth level to be a cloud. It could be caused only by one thing — riders. Realization hit him with sudden force. The Comanches! They had discovered their escape. They were on the trail. He wheeled to Burke and the others.

"Mount up!" he shouted, and started for his pony.

There was a moment of stunned silence at Ricker's unexpected harshness, and then all rushed to comply with his command.

"Comanches?" Burke shouted as he pulled himself onto the saddle.

For answer Dan pointed to the dust roll. He saw the old lawman's jaw clamp shut. Marfa Talbot stared, her features pulled into a frown. Beyond her Gorman was grim.

Ricker wished he had taken time to snatch up the third Comanche guard's rifle when he had struck the man down. But the brave's yell had startled him, filled him with the need to get the others away from the corral and the camp as quickly as possible. A weapon in the hands of Jack Gorman, despite later troublesome possibilities, would be a welcome addition.

There was no point in thinking of it now. Dan dug his heels into the pony's flanks, and they moved off the slope at a trot. When they reached the bottom of the grade they broke the tired horses into a lope, still keeping to the base of the low hills. There was little sense in trying to stay out of sight; the dust lifted by their passage would be as apparent to the Comancheros and Indians as theirs had been to them.

They rushed on, not halting to rest. Dan kept a constant watch on their back trail and quickly saw that they were losing ground. The yellowish pall was growing larger, more definite. The renegades and their Indian allies, not hampered in any way, were closing the gap with alarming speed.

Near midmorning the pursuers were in sight. There were at least two dozen in the party, perhaps a few more flung to either flank. About half, Dan saw, were Comancheros. As Burke had said, they were not taking kindly to losing their prizes.

They rode on, not sparing their suffering horses. Doherty's could not be far away, Ricker knew, unless he had somehow misjudged and overshot the settlement. He yelled that question at Gorman.

Jack shook his head, his face set to grim lines of worry and fear. "Don't know this country around here!" he shouted back. "Done my riding farther north."

Ricker threw a glance to the rear. The Comanches were distinct now, lean, dark shapes crouched low over their ponies. The Comancheros were slightly to the rear, being outdistanced by the more expert Indians. Dan turned his attention ahead. They were racing down a long, gentle slope into a wide valley.

"There's smoke!" Burke cried suddenly and pointed to the north.

Relief surged through Ricker at the lawman's words. He swung his eyes to the north rim of the valley. A thin stream of smoke trickled up into the sky.

"Doherty's!" he shouted. "Has to be!"

He cast another look at the oncoming Comanches. They were nearer but still well beyond rifle range. Ricker calculated their chances. If they could reach the far ridge of the swale, if the horses could stand the thundering pace until they gained the summit — they might make it. Likely Doherty's place would be in view then, and the Comanches would abandon the chase.

He touched the straining horses with a critical appraisal. They were about done for. Gorman's black and Burke's buckskin seemed to be standing it best of all. The sorrel was not too bad, his load being light. But the thin, poorly fed and cared-for Indian ponies would not last much longer.

They reached the bottom of the grassy valley and started up the opposing grade. The horses faltered noticeably when they hit the climb, but struggled on. Dan threw a look at the Comanches. They were streaming over the summit behind. At once several of the Indians began to shoot, the reports hollow and echoing on the hot, dry air. The bullets fell short.

Halfway up to the ridge, the Comanches opened up again. Dan saw spurts of sand where the slugs dug into the ground, only paces back now. He twisted about on his pony and raised his rifle. Aiming above the nearest Indian, he squeezed off a shot. The bullet was close. He saw the Comanche flinch and swerve to one side. Burke, hearing Ricker shoot, slowed, began to fall back.

Dan waved him on. "Keep going! I'll try to turn them."

The old lawman nodded and resumed the climb, pulling in beside Gorman. Burke, looking forward to a successful escape from the renegades, was now taking precautions where Gorman was concerned.

More gunshots began to hammer through the late-morning heat. Dan heard the drone of lead, but most of it fell short. The Comancheros, he saw, were fading from the chase. Only two or three were among the riders charging across the floor of the valley.

Dan continued to lever an occasional shot at the Indians, using his ammunition sparingly. Once on the ridge he could wheel and make a stand while the others hurried on to safety at Doherty's. He glanced ahead. The rim was only yards away. Already Jack and his big horse were silhouetted against the sky. They were almost in the clear.

Ricker centered his attention on the Comanches. Five riders were pounding up the slope — one of them Largo, another Chino, the Comanchero leader. The Indian chief was out in front of the others. He was driving hard, hammering frantically at the flanks of his pony with his heels. His mouth gaped open, and the sound of his yelling was high-pitched and weird. The braves behind him were silent and maintained an intermittent fire. Chino seemed bent only on keeping pace with the Comanches.

Abruptly Ricker found himself on the crest of the ridge. Below, strung out at a dead run for Doherty's, now a half a mile distant, were Marfa, Burke, and Gorman. Dan grinned tightly, hauled his pony to a stop, and wheeled about. The advantage was his. He looked down at Largo and the others. They were less than a hundred yards away.

Ignoring the bullets of the Comanches, Ricker brought his rifle to his shoulder. He steadied himself and took close aim. When the gun bucked he saw Largo jolt and sway to the side. The Indian caught himself. His bared teeth gleamed in the hot sunlight as he struggled to lift his rifle. There was no strength in his arms. He dropped the weapon suddenly and clawed at his horse's mane to save himself from falling. The pony slowed and began to turn.

Taking his time, Ricker drew a bead on the Comanche to the left of the chief and pressed off a shot. The brave went backward off his mount as the heavy slug smashed into his breast. Dan pivoted fast. He wanted a chance at Chino, but the Comanchero had spun about and was racing headlong back down the slope. Ricker threw a shot at him, ignoring the distance. It missed, as he had known it would. Swearing softly, he came back to face the remaining braves. They too had cut off and were plunging for the valley floor. Largo, clinging desperately to his horse, followed.

A hard grin broke Ricker's tightly compressed lips. They'd made it — and it would end there insofar as the Comanches were concerned. With Chino and his renegades it could be something else again; they might not give it up.

But such was of little, if any, concern to him. Once they pulled into Doherty's, he could wash his hands of the unwanted responsibility that had dropped into his lap. All he need think of was the food, water, and good bed that awaited him there. Sighing, he wheeled and started down the long grade.

# CHAPTER
# EIGHT

Doherty's place consisted of a large, ramshackle building fronted by a full-width porch that had several holes in its sagging roof. Numerous small sheds, a few broken-down wagons, and a hulking barn surrounded by corrals stood at the rear. Off to one side were a half a dozen one-room shacks that apparently were the homes of those who worked for the freighter.

A number of roughly dressed men and washed-out-looking women had gathered on the porch, attracted by the shooting and the sight of the party racing down from the ridge. They watched in silence as Ricker and the others rode onto the hardpack and pulled up to the hitch rail.

"Hey there, Gabe!" Gorman shouted genially. "Sure am glad to be looking at you!"

Doherty, a bearded man somewhere in his fifties and dressed in ragged, dirty overalls and sodbuster shoes, shuffled forward and leaned up against one of the porch supports. He was bald, and his reddish brows and light-colored eyes gave him the appearance of having been peeled. At Gorman's greeting he grinned faintly, but he held his glance on Burke.

"Howdy, Jack," he said finally. "What was all the shootin'? Comanches?"

Gorman nodded. "And Comancheros. Had us penned up, but we managed to get loose."

Doherty bobbed his round head. "They been raisin' hell in these parts lately. Who's your friends?"

Gorman waved carelessly in the direction of Marfa and Ricker. "Couple o' pilgrims I ran into. Lady's from back east somewheres. Comanches got her folks. Ricker — well, don't rightly know where he hails from. This here," he added, turning to Burke, "happens to be the marshal of Canyon City. Reckon you could say I'm his guest."

"Prisoner," Burke said dryly.

Ricker dropped from his pony, moved to the sorrel, and helped Marfa dismount, fully aware of the hard, raking interest the loafers on the gallery showed in the girl. As she turned to face them several low whistles lifted. Anger stirred Dan Ricker.

Gorman said, "Treat the lady right now, boys. Expect she's mighty hungry and tired."

One of the teamsters stepped up, swept off his hat, and bowed low. "Sister, I'd be right pleased to buy you a meal — any time."

A laugh went up. Another man shouldered the speaker aside. "Lady, for a couple of favors — I'll just up and buy you anything you want!"

More laughter sounded. Marfa looked appealingly at Ricker. There was a paleness showing beneath her light tan, and he realized with a start that she was afraid. She had displayed no fear at the Indian camp, but now it was apparent — and for good reason.

She was utterly alone. Burke and Gorman would continue to Canyon City. He would be going his way to Oregon. Marfa was stranded; alone, friendless, and without funds in a rat's nest of idle hardcase muleskinners.

"Be enough of that," he snapped, throwing his words at the teamster. "The lady's with me."

The first man bristled. He ducked his head at Jack Gorman. "That ain't what he said . . ."

"I don't give a damn what he said," Ricker snarled. "And if I hear any more remarks passed at the lady there'll be trouble. Understand?"

The teamster held his pose for a long minute; then, under Ricker's hard, thrusting glare, he wilted and turned away. Dan swung his attention to Doherty.

"Got a couple of rooms? And we'll be eating here."

Doherty shrugged. "I got the rooms and the grub if you've got the price. Supper'll be about dark." He looked at Gorman. "You wantin' keep, too?"

Gorman's eyes were on a lean, sandy-haired rider who had come from the interior of the building and now slumped indolently against the door frame, hand resting on the butt of his low-slung pistol. But if he were an acquaintance of Gorman's he gave no sign.

"What about it, Jack?" Doherty asked again.

"We'll be stayin' — for a couple of hours," Burke answered. "Like somethin' to eat right now, and grub for the trail."

Doherty stared at Gorman. "That right?"

Jack shifted lazily. "He's calling the shots."

Doherty considered that and nodded. Ricker reached into his pocket for some loose coins. It would be several hours until dark; Marfa and he could use some food too. The sandy-haired puncher moved out to the edge of the porch. Burke's head came up sharply. He gave him a narrow-eyed scrutiny. Dan paused.

Gorman, a crooked smile on his lips, looked at the lawman. "It all right if I climb down, Marshal?"

Burke said, "It's all right. But do it slow and easy. Just keep rememberin' this rifle's drillin' you dead center."

Dan handed the coins to Marfa. "Going to be a while before we get a meal. Go inside and buy us a few things we can work on in the meantime. I'll be out back taking care of the horses."

Marfa cupped the coins in her palm and glanced hesitantly toward the porch.

Ricker shook his head. "They won't bother you now. If somebody does, sing out."

She gave him a taut smile and started for the doorway. Ricker remained motionless, watching until she had crossed the porch and entered the shadowy depths of the building. Then, gathering up the reins of the sorrel and the halter rope of the Indian pony, he headed for the corral. Ben Burke's knife-edged voice halted him.

"Stand clear, mister!"

Dan pivoted, alert for trouble. The lawman was directing his words to the sandy-haired gunman, now off the porch and in the yard.

"Who are you?" There was suspicion in Burke's tone.

The puncher moved his shoulders slightly and fell back a step. "Don't figure it's none of your business, but I'm Clint Sandusky."

"Everything's my business right now," Burke snapped. "Keep your distance."

Dan Ricker relaxed, turned, and continued on. He reached the corner of Doherty's and led the horses toward an open shed near the corral where he could see hay piled in a manger. The water trough caught his notice and he veered to it. While the animals slaked their thirst, he satisfied his own needs, mentally reminding himself to buy a new canteen from Doherty before he moved on. When the horses had finished, he crossed the yard to the leanto.

There was a small quantity of bran in the bin along with the hay, and the horses began to feed at once. Dan stepped to the sorrel and began to remove his gear. At that moment Marfa Talbot appeared. She was carrying a loaf of fresh bread, a jar of coffee, and some other items of food.

Ricker abandoned his chore to aid her. She smiled as he came up, this time more freely.

"Couldn't find much to buy," she said. "Bread, a little dried meat, and fresh peaches. I'm afraid the coffee's not very hot."

"It'll do fine," Ricker said, taking the bread and the jar of coffee. "Have any trouble?"

"None," she said. "I — I want to thank you — for everything."

"Forget it," he said gruffly.

They moved in under the roof of the open shed. Dan dragged in an empty nail keg for her to sit on, while he contented himself by squatting on his heels, back to the plank wall. They began to eat immediately, wasting no time on conversation.

He was thinking about her. That she could not remain at Doherty's had already been decided in his mind. Leaving her there would be the same as throwing a helpless lamb to a pack of wolves.

Such left two alternatives — persuade her to ride on to Canyon City with Burke and Gorman, which could prove dangerous if Jack's promise of deliverance by his family materialized; or take her on with him and look after her until they reached a town.

He thrashed both ideas about in his mind slowly, angrily, resentful that the decision was his. Finally, he concluded that the only answer was to keep Marfa with him. Settling on that, he swore inwardly. He had thought he would be free of responsibility when they reached Doherty's; he was far from it.

"A Goddamn nursemaid," he muttered.

Marfa glanced at him. "Did you say something?"

Ricker looked down so that she would not see the fury simmering in his eyes. "Nothing," he said, but there was no hiding the disgust in his tone.

He rose, tossed away a scrap of bread, dusted his palms. After a moment he turned and studied her thoughtfully. A stray lock of her hair had come loose and now trailed down across her forehead. She brushed it back, unaware of his attention.

**68**

"Expect you'll have to stick with me a while longer," he said.

She looked up inquiringly. "Why?"

"I can't leave you here," Ricker said, annoyed. "You got a sample of what it would be like when we rode in."

Her face was drawn, and she appeared tired and dusty in the faded, worn shirt and pants she had salvaged from her father's effects. "I suppose not. Maybe I could go on to Canyon City with the marshal."

"Burke's expecting trouble. That Gorman crowd plays rough, and you could get hurt — and I doubt if you'd be much better off with the Gormans than you would be here with these teamsters."

She sighed wearily and shook her head. "Things happen so fast . . . so — so completely. Two weeks ago I had a family, a mother and a father. We were moving west, had high hopes for a new life somewhere in Arizona. I was going to teach school, or maybe open a shop of some sort. Now there's nothing. Nothing left, nothing to look forward to."

Ricker's hard features softened. His tone relented. "Don't give up yet. We'll keep going until we reach a town. Then I'll make arrangements for you to get back to your relatives in the East."

She shook her head. "Maybe I shouldn't be proud, but I don't want charity. If you'll just help me get to a town, I'll find a job and look out for myself."

"However you want it," he said, his manner again abrupt. He glanced toward Doherty's ungainly building. "Forgot to say *adios* to Burke. Expect I'd better do that before he pulls out."

"When I came from the store they were sitting on the porch eating," she said. "Some man was watering their horses."

"Reckon they're about ready then," Dan said, reaching for his cigarette makings.

She watched him for a moment, then asked, "Why is he taking Jack Gorman to Canyon City? What did he do?"

"Killed a man," Ricker said.

"Was it over a woman?"

"Seems so —"

The sudden crack of two quick gunshots shattered the afternoon hush. Dan whirled. The reports had sounded as though they came from the front of Doherty's. His first thought was of Comanches — or possibly the Comancheros. But there was no yelling, no churning dust. Then he heard the hard pound of a horse racing off to the east. Face grim, he flung a glance at Marfa, now upright and staring at him. Jerking his rifle from its boot, he wheeled.

"Stay here," he yelled, and started for the yard at a run.

# CHAPTER
# NINE

When he reached the forward corner of Doherty's store, Ricker stopped. He raised his rifle, and observing the old axiom never to burst suddenly onto the scene of a shooting, he eased into the open.

In one sweeping glance he took it in. Ben Burke lay face down in the yard. On his back were twin spreading bloodstains. Beyond him stood the puncher named Sandusky. Doherty and the teamsters and women he had seen earlier were clustered on the porch.

Far to the east, almost beyond the point of recognition, was Jack Gorman, astride his huge black horse and riding fast.

Face taut, Ricker strode to the side of the fallen lawman. He knelt and rolled Burke to his back. Death had been sudden and unexpected. It was all there, written on the marshal's contorted features. Dan rose and pivoted to Doherty. A hot, unreasoning anger was pushing through him.

"Was it Gorman?"

The freighter shook his head. A man standing a few paces to his side said, "Jack got a gun and —"

"Shut up, Earl!" Doherty growled. "We don't know nothin' about this."

"Two bullets — in the back," Ricker said, scorn riding his tone. "Gorman's a brave man." He swept the gathering with his glance. "Where'd he get a gun?"

Doherty shrugged. "How the hell should I know? Maybe he had it hid on him."

That would be far from truth. Burke was an experienced lawman and a careful one. He would not overlook a concealed weapon, particularly where Jack Gorman was concerned. Besides, Jack would have used it earlier at the Indian camp. Ricker swore in disgust.

"Makes no difference now — Burke's dead. Thing to do is go after Jack before he can get away. Start making up a posse."

Doherty did not stir. He stared at Dan for several moments, turned his head, and spat.

"Not much, we ain't," he said. "We're not havin' anythin' to do with it."

"What!" Ricker exploded. "That man's a murderer — a killer!"

"That man," the freighter said slowly and distinctly, "is old Frank Gorman's boy."

"So?"

"So — if you've got a lick of sense, you'll keep your nose out of it, same as we're doin'. Nobody in his right mind is goin' to rile Frank Gorman."

From somewhere in Dan's memory Ben Burke's voice made itself heard: "It's every man's bounden duty to see law's upheld." He had not given the old marshal's words much thought at the time; now they took on real meaning.

"That's got nothing to do with it," Ricker said sharply. "Gorman or not, Jack's got to be brought in. He's been sentenced to hang for one killing. This makes it twice as necessary."

"This don't make nothin'," Clint Sandusky said, moving in nearer. "And you'd better listen to Gabe, friend, or you're liable to wake up holdin' a catamount by the ear."

Dan came half-about and faced the hard-eyed man. Clint, he recalled, had been the one Burke warned to stand clear. He could have had justifiable suspicions where the puncher was concerned.

"Maybe. You some kind of special friend of the Gormans'?"

"Could be. Worked for old Frank once."

Ricker's gaze dropped to the empty holster at Sandusky's hip. "Guess I know now where Jack got the gun."

Clint laughed and feigned surprise. He allowed his hand to drop to the naked leather. "Well — what d'you think of that? Jack must've snatched my iron when I wasn't lookin'."

Sandusky was making it all sound like a big joke, and the crowd on Doherty's porch was responding with nods and smiles.

"You're a liar," Dan said coldly. "My guess is you slipped it to him when the marshal's back was turned."

Sandusky bristled and drew himself up. "You callin' me a liar?"

"You heard me. And I'll tell you something else — it makes you a part of the murder."

73

Sandusky's voice was husky. "You talk mighty big, knowin' I ain't packin' a gun."

"You're a liar, with or without one," Dan said, "and not worth wasting time on — not while Gorman's getting away." He swung his attention to the porch. "I want a posse. Any man here with guts enough to ride with me?"

There was no answer. Ricker touched each one with a contemptuous glance.

"Burke was a hell of a good lawman — and he deserved better than being shot in the back. It's too bad he had to die for bastards like you, for without him and his kind this country would be crawling with outlaws and killers."

Sandusky scratched at his jaw. "You're doin' a lot of preachin' for a pilgrim. You sure you ain't a deputy or somethin'?"

"Every man's a deputy when it comes to upholding the law — according to Burke. Never gave it much thought until now, but I reckon he was right. And there was something else he said that makes sense — that there's too many kings in Texas. He meant men like Frank Gorman. Your standing there afraid to do something that might rile Gorman proves he knew what he was talking about."

Ricker paused, vaguely disturbed by the words coming from his own throat. His was, and always had been, a policy of staying out of other people's business — yet here he was wading straight into an affair better left to Burke's brother lawmen. But somehow it seemed the right thing to do.

74

"You keep figuring the way you are and someday you won't have anything. You'll be nothing — no more than dirt on Gorman's boots. And every time he sees you, he'll expect you to squat and lick them clean. That's what you can figure on if you keep knuckling under."

Dan paused. Doherty and the others continued to stare at him from wooden faces. "I'm asking once more — how about that posse?"

There was only silence. Clint Sandusky laughed, the only sound in the hot, dry hush.

Ricker swore and bobbed his head. "All right. I'll go it alone."

He leaned over Burke's lifeless body and removed the pin from the lawman's vest. As he straightened he saw Marfa standing at the corner of Doherty's building watching him. She had a curious, almost proud smile on her lips. He frowned at her presence as he pinned the star onto his shirt.

"Burke offered me a deputy job back along the trail. Turned it down, but I've changed my mind. I'm taking it."

"The hell you are!" Sandusky yelled and rushed forward.

Dan had only time enough to whirl. Sandusky's shoulder crashed into his own. The rifle flew from his grasp at the impact, and they went down hard into the dust.

# CHAPTER
# TEN

He struck the ground with Sandusky's full weight upon him. An oath ripped from his lips, and he smashed savagely at the man's jaw.

His fist connected with a dull, meaty thud. Clint heaved to one side. Instantly Ricker rolled clear and bounded to his feet. Sandusky, light as a cat, was up and closing in.

Dan pivoted and lashed out. His fist caught Clint low on the head, shook him, rocked him off balance. The puncher cursed and reached out with both hands. Ricker dodged the clawing fingers and drove two quick blows to Clint's belly. The puncher gasped with pain, halted flat-footed.

Ricker, thoroughly aroused and wholly angered by the turn of events that had inexplicably tangled him in their web, rushed in, arms driving like pistons. His knuckles drilled into Sandusky mercilessly. The tall man began to fall back, wilting under the relentless hammering.

Clint sagged to one knee — and then to the other. His shaggy head dropped forward between slumped shoulders. Ricker paused, his chest heaving, his body trembling with fury and exertion. He glared at Sandusky.

"You through?"

The puncher made no reply. Dan took a step nearer. "You hear me? You had eno—"

"Hell with you!" Sandusky yelled, and lunged.

He caught Ricker around the legs, dragged him to the ground again. Then he lurched forward and spreadeagled Dan with his body.

"I ain't even started good!" he gritted. "When I get through with you, you'll wish you'd never come across me!"

He brought his knee up, driving it deep into Dan's unprotected side. Ricker winced with pain as he struggled to dislodge Clint. Sandusky retaliated with a vicious chop to the neck with the heel of his hand.

Blind rage roared through Ricker. He kicked one leg free, doubled it, jerked upward. His knee caught Sandusky under the arm, threw him to one side. Putting all his strength into the effort, Dan got his right arm loose and drew back. He struck downward, aiming for Sandusky's ear.

The blow went true. Clint howled and pulled away. Ricker used his knee again, and when Clint was off-center, he heaved the man aside. Dan rolled away, but Sandusky was after him instantly. Ricker felt the toe of Sandusky's boot drive into his ribs as he fought to get clear. Clint, amazingly fast for a big man, gave him no chance to rise.

Dan took a second brutal smash into his ribs. A little harder and he would have had some broken bones to think about. But there was no time to consider possibilities. Sandusky had murder in his eyes. Unless Dan gained the upper hand again, he was as good as dead.

Ricker continued to roll, to twist and turn. He had a fleeting glimpse through the hazy dust of the hitchrack just ahead. Burke's horse, still tied to the bar, was shying nervously. Dan pivoted on his back and rolled toward the rack, purposely drawing himself under the wooden framework.

Sandusky halted briefly, yelled something, and tried to reach over the pole and grasp Ricker's hair. Dan, coming to a sitting position, dodged the puncher's groping fingers and seized him by the wrists. He threw all his weight into a quick jerk. Sandusky buckled across the bar. The dry, rotted pole snapped, and the tall man crashed to the hardpack.

Dan was up and had Sandusky by the shirt collar before the puncher knew what was happening. He kicked aside the shattered rack and started to pull the puncher back into the open yard. The cloth gave way under the strain and came loose in a ragged strip.

Not hesitating, Dan seized Sandusky by the hair, dragged the screaming, cursing man a half a dozen steps, and halted! He drew him partly upright and swung a roundhouse blow to the man's chin, which popped like a muleskinner's whip.

Clint went down like a lead weight. Ricker reached for Sandusky's hair again, pulled him up, drove another blow to the jaw. This time Sandusky did not stir or make the slightest sound as he sprawled in the dust. He was completely out.

Plastered with dirt, his body smarting from Clint's kicks and blows, Dan Ricker staggered back. He was sucking deep for breath, and his lungs seemed about to burst. Anger still burned through him, clouding his eyes with a yellow fog. He stooped down, scooped up his gun, and wheeled to the men on the porch.

"If any . . . of you . . . figures to stop me . . . start now!"

His furious glance swept across them all. None made any reply or move toward accepting the challenge.

Ricker was breathing easier, more normally. He nodded. "Just keep playing it smart and you'll have no trouble . . . Marfa!"

"I'm here," she called in a breathless voice from the corner of the building.

"Bring my sorrel around. Don't bother with the pony — you can ride the marshal's buckskin. Hurry."

From the tail of his eye he saw her disappear. He beckoned to the freighter. "You — Doherty. Come here."

The bald-headed man hesitated, then came off the porch slowly. He halted in front of Ricker. "What's on your mind?"

"Your gun — I'm buying it, belt and all. Take it off."

Doherty removed his equipment and passed it to Dan. Marfa appeared, leading the sorrel. She halted a few steps from him. Dan handed her the rifle and motioned at Doherty.

"Keep it on him. If he moves, pull the trigger. He's our insurance."

She nodded and, white-faced, took the weapon into her hands. Ricker strapped on Doherty's gun and reached into his pocket for a gold piece. He dropped it into the freighter's shirt pocket.

"More'n the outfit's worth, but I don't have time to argue."

He wheeled to the sorrel and pulled tight the cinch he had loosened earlier. He moved then to the rack, released Burke's horse, and led him back. Taking the rifle from Marfa he thrust the reins into her hands.

"Mount up."

She climbed onto the buckskin. The stirrups were too long. She pushed her toes into the leather loops that supported the wood. Giving her back the rifle, Dan swung onto the sorrel. He looked down at the sweating Gabe Doherty.

"We're riding out of here — and you're walking ahead of us till we reach that stand of brush. My gun's pointed straight at your head. If any of your friends take a notion to stop us, you're a dead man. That plain enough?"

"Plain enough," Doherty said grudgingly. He turned his face to the porch. "You heard him. Don't go tryin' nothin'."

Dan swept the crowd with his glance, pulled the sorrel about, and crowded him against Doherty. "All right; let's go," he said.

# CHAPTER
# ELEVEN

Leaving Doherty's, Jack Gorman had fled eastward, toward the Double Diamond spread. Apparently he was not planning to seek sanctuary in Mexico again, preferring instead the protective shadow of his father.

Abandoning Doherty once they reached the safety of the brush, Ricker and Marfa Talbot urged their mounts to a lope and struck off on a course thought by Dan to be the one taken by the outlaw. It could be a long, hard ride — and a dangerous one — and he regretted being compelled to take the girl with him. But there had been no choice.

He slid a glance at her, a few paces to his left. She rode well, but the slight sag of her body bespoke her weariness. He hoped, for her sake, that they could overtake Gorman soon; then they could halt and she could get some rest.

He looked back over his shoulder toward Doherty's, but a roll in the land now hid it from view. He was not concerned with the freighter and his men; it was a hundred to one that they would not take it upon themselves to follow; but Clint Sandusky was something else.

He was a friend of the Gormans'. That he had supplied Jack with the gun that had spelled death for Ben Burke was unquestionable — and that he would do more to aid him was just as sure. The only question in Dan's mind was whether the puncher would come in search of him or would head for the Double Diamond to get the rest of the Gormans.

There were no riders in sight anywhere, and Ricker took some comfort from that. Either Sandusky was still recovering from the beating he had taken, or he was a bit reluctant to get started. And of course, it could be that he had taken a different route, one not visible to Ricker. Dan decided that there was nothing gained in speculating, that all he could do was wait and watch.

He cast a look at the sun. There were not many more hours of daylight remaining. He must locate Jack soon, or his task would be tripled. Once night closed in over the broad, rolling plains and hills, he would be searching blind, and his chances of overtaking Gorman before he could reach the Double Diamond would be seriously diminished.

He touched Marfa again with his eyes. If only he didn't have her along to worry about . . . She was bound to slow him down, and if the situation got tight, he would have to think first of her and her safety and then of what must be done.

She turned to him in that moment, her face calm. She lifted her arm and pointed ahead. Ricker swung his glance about and stiffened. Jack Gorman, little more than a dot in the distance, was laboring slowly up a long grade. The black he rode was laboring wearily.

Gorman had pushed him hard when he left Doherty's, and now the big gelding was about down. He would have to stop soon.

Ricker swerved in nearer to Marfa and grinned at her. "Luck's running our way. Soon as I get my hands on Gorman we'll make camp and you can rest. Too bad we didn't bring along that grub you bought."

She pointed to his saddlebags. "It's in there — what was left of it. And we've got plenty of water," she added, lifting Burke's canteen.

Dan smiled again. Marfa Talbot was no ordinary woman; she had a good head on her shoulders — and used it.

He put his attention again on Gorman. The outlaw was climbing a deep saddle that lay between two fairly high hills. On the opposite side the swale dropped again and became once more a long, somewhat narrow valley that continued on into the east. Apparently Jack, wanting to keep below the horizon as much as possible, intended to follow the depression until it petered out.

As they pressed on in the wake of the outlaw, Dan studied the land before him, got it all firmly fixed in his mind. If he figured right, once Gorman topped the saddle and dropped off onto the opposite slope, he would call a halt. The black would have to rest, and Jack, the ridge behind him, would consider it a safe place to stop.

Such would fit neatly into Ricker's plan. By circling around the hills, he could cut in on Gorman from the east. He would not be expecting anyone from that point, and it should be easy to work in close and take the outlaw without gunplay. He turned to Marfa, outlined his scheme to her.

"Be best for you to keep back," he added when she signified her understanding. "And if anything goes wrong, head north. Canyon City's up that way, somewhere."

"I can help," she said, laying her hand on the butt of the rifle riding in the boot.

He had given it to her back at Doherty's and had forgotten about it. He doubted if there were more than three or four cartridges in it.

"You may need it yourself," he said. "I'll make out."

Immediately he swung off the slight ridge they had been following, and with Marfa a few paces behind, he began to circle the hill. Near dark they halted in a deep arroyo. By his calculations they should be abreast of Gorman, with only the shoulder of the hill separating them.

Leaving Marfa with the horses, he climbed the grade. Once on the crest, he dropped to his belly and crawled forward until he could look down into the swale. Disappointment rocked him. The hollow was empty. He pulled himself upright and glanced toward the top of the saddle. Nothing scarred the smooth, grassy slopes of the bow.

And then motion near the foot of the grade caught Dan Ricker's eye. He edged forward that he might have a better view. Relief claimed him. He had overshot the outlaw. Gorman was sitting on the bank of an arroyo less than a quarter mile away. His black gelding, head low, stood nearby.

Dan withdrew quickly. Keeping low, he doubled back, maintaining a safe distance between himself and the hollow. When he was at a point he judged to be directly opposite the arroyo where Gorman rested, he cut in. He moved quietly, hopeful of taking the outlaw by surprise. Jack had Sandusky's gun. There would be three, perhaps four cartridges in its cylinder. He doubted if Gorman had taken time to procure more ammunition before he fled.

But Ricker was determined to avoid gunplay if possible. Shooting could attract others — and they were probably near, possibly even on, Double Diamond range.

Again reaching the top of the rise, Ricker removed his hat. He worked his way in through the clumps of creosote bush and yellow snakeweed until he could look down into the hollow. He had figured right this time. Jack was below him, less than a hundred yards distant.

Crouched, he started down the grade, catfooting each step. Halfway down he paused and drew his pistol. Gorman, back to him, was intent on something in the distance. Dan pressed on, calling on every ounce of his skill to move soundlessly. Thirty yards . . . twenty. He would wait until no more than a dozen paces separated them, then make his rush. With luck he would take Gorman off-guard, be on him before he could react.

Ricker continued, now almost creeping. Jack stirred, shifting his attention to the black. He cursed the horse unreasonably for its spent condition, gained some sort of release from the display of temper, and settled back again. Dan did not halt.

Fifteen yards . . .

Ricker's nerves were taut as steel piano wires. Sweat beaded his face, trickled down his neck, bathed him. Somewhere high above him, an eagle screeched, but he did not look up. A little more . . . a little closer . . . then make the rush.

Suddenly Ricker heard the hammer of a horse coming down the swale at a dead run. A gunshot smashed the late-afternoon stillness. Sand spurted over Dan's boots as a bullet dug into the ground at his feet. Then a voice — Clint Sandusky's voice — reached him.

"Jack — look out! Behind you!"

# CHAPTER
# TWELVE

Ricker plunged forward and snapped a hasty shot at the oncoming Sandusky. The gunman flinched, swerving his pinto horse sharply. Gorman's pistol blasted, almost in Dan's face, it seemed, but he charged on. The outlaw was dead ahead. Ricker lowered his shoulder and he caught Gorman in the chest, knocking him backward onto the arroyo bank.

Off-balance, Dan fought to stay on his feet. He fell to one knee, but he got off another shot at Sandusky. He heard the thud of the bullet as it hit some part of the puncher's saddle, listened to its wild scream as it ricocheted off into space. The pinto shied violently, almost spilling Sandusky from its back, reared, then struck down the slope with its rider swaying uncertainly on his perch.

Breathing heavily, anger roaring through him, Dan wheeled to Gorman. The outlaw was on his hands and knees endeavoring to recover his revolver, jolted from his grasp at the collision. Ricker leaped toward him and kicked the weapon off into the brush.

"Get up, damn you!" he yelled.

As Gorman struggled to rise, Dan threw a glance at Sandusky. The pinto was just topping a rise to the east, going away fast. Clint was hunched over his saddle, holding his arm. He was out of it — at least for a time.

"Grab those reins," Ricker ordered. "We're getting out of here."

Gorman reached for the black's leathers, then paused stubbornly. "Who says so? You ain't the law. That tin badge you're wearing don't mean —"

"Means I took over where Burke left off," Dan said harshly. "We're going on to Canyon City."

"What kind of authority you —"

"This kind," Dan said, wagging the revolver in his hand suggestively.

Gorman's shoulders slumped. "You won't get far. Clint's on his way right now to the ranch. He'll be coming back with Pa and my brothers."

"They'll have to find us," Ricker said, shoving Gorman roughly down the grade. "Get moving."

The outlaw stumbled, righted himself, started off leading the spent black. After a few steps, he looked back at Ricker.

"You aiming to walk to Canyon City?"

"My horse is on the other side of the hill," Dan said.

They moved up the incline and dropped off onto the other side. Marfa Talbot was sitting on a low bench of rock. She rose to meet them, relief plain on her face.

"I heard shooting," she said as they came up to her.

Ricker shook his head. "No damage. But it means we'll have to keep going. Gorman's friend's gone after his pa and big brothers."

Jack was studying her, a half smile on his face. "Sort of surprised to see you trailing along with him," he said. "Makes it nice — real nice."

Marfa lowered her head. Ricker wheeled and angrily pushed Gorman toward his horse. "Mount up," he snarled.

Gorman laughed and swung onto his saddle. He watched as Dan procured a short length of rope from his saddlebags. Without hesitation he put his arms behind his back and crossed his wrists.

"You're just wasting your time, tying me up," he said. "Pa'll be here soon. And anyway, this horse of mine ain't going far."

"He'll last a few miles," Dan said, "and that's all I need."

"Still catch up with us," Jack persisted. "And when they do you'll wish you'd never seen this part of Texas."

Ricker finished linking the outlaw's wrists. He sighed wearily. "Already wishing that. I'm plenty tired of it — and you."

He turned to Marfa. She was already on the buckskin. He moved to his own horse, stepped to the saddle.

"If you're feeling that way, then forget this, pull out," Gorman said. "You can try, but you won't ever get me to Canyon City. Burke figured he could — but he's dead. You'll end up the same way."

"I don't plan on ending up the way Burke did," Dan said. "Let's go."

They moved off in silence, Marfa in the lead, followed by Gorman and then Ricker. He had not bothered to tie a lead rope on the outlaw's black. The big gelding was too beat to make a break, and it was easier traveling in this manner. He could keep an eye on Gorman and watch their back trail better from that position.

He did take the precaution of riding with his pistol ready in his hand. They were on Double Diamond range, he was certain, and there was the possibility of blundering into some of Gorman's hired hands. If such occurred he wanted to be set; Ben Burke had paid his penalty for a moment's unwariness, and Dan was determined not to be caught in the same way.

Shortly after nightfall Ricker called a halt in a shallow bowl of land well studded by brush. Marfa started to dismount, but he stopped her.

"Be here only a couple of minutes," he said. "Stay on your horse."

She was near exhaustion. She settled back on her saddle, staring at him in a wondering, almost stupid way. He shook his head, again impatient with the misfortune that had placed her in his care. Coming off his sorrel, he pulled the brush jacket he carried from the roll behind the cantle of his saddle.

He then removed Gorman's, and taking the two garments, he walked out into the center of the coulée. He halted there and glanced around. Selecting two clumps of brush of proper size, he draped the jackets over them and buttoned them into place. A short distance away from the dummies, he gathered a fairly large pile of dry sticks and green brush and built a fire, arranging the wood so that it would burn for a considerable time.

That completed, he dropped back a few yards to survey his work. In the darkness, and at a distance, the camp appeared natural enough. To anyone attracted by the fire's glow and looking on from one of the nearby hills, the clothed bushes resembled men hunkered near the flames.

He discovered a rotting mesquite stump on his way back to the horses, and adding this to the fire, he climbed back onto the sorrel. Jack Gorman's jeering voice grated on his ears.

"You think your fake camp's going to fool Pa, you've got another guess coming."

"It'll fool him long enough to put us plenty far ahead," Dan replied. "Time he works himself in and finds out for sure, we ought to be miles from here." He nodded to Marfa. "Go ahead. We'll stop and rest as soon as it's safe."

She moved off at once, and they dropped into the pattern they had previously observed. Gorman twisted on his saddle.

"Won't make any difference. They'll be riding fresh horses. They'll catch up."

"I'll be ready," Ricker said tiredly.

They rode slowly on over the flats and low hills, silver now under a bright moon. The night was warm, filled with the lonely sounds of darkness — a distant coyote, softly calling birds, the muted click of insects.

Once, Dan heard a gunshot far to the west, but it had no meaning for him. When trouble came it would come rushing in from the east, or possibly the south, depending upon how well his ruse worked. He hoped the Gormans would fall for it. It could mean as much as an extra hour in their flight — and an hour could spell the difference between life and death.

"Ricker . . ."

At Gorman's voice, Dan looked up. "Yeh?"

"Was just thinking — how about a deal? I can pay you plenty. Three, maybe four hundred dollars. All you got to do is forget Canyon City. Cut me loose, and we'll all head for the ranch. Pa'll pay — if I tell him to."

"You're mighty free with his money . . ."

"Could even get it up to five hundred — and you better be remembering that you won't collect a cent reward for taking me in. Not a red cent. Pa'll be plenty riled, but I can square it with him. He'll pay you off."

"With a sixgun," Ricker said. "I know the kind of man your pa is. I've done business with them before."

"Not if I give you my word."

Dan laughed scornfully. "Word of a man who shot down an unarmed homesteader? One who put two bullets into a lawman's back? Your word's not worth a puff of sand."

"By God, the Gorman word's always good!" Jack shouted. "Goddammit, Ricker, listen to me! I'm offering you your life — and maybe the lady's, too! It'll be hell if Pa cuts loose on you. And five hundred cash to boot — enough money to last you quite a spell."

"Don't think I'd sleep good at night," Ricker said mildly, deliberately egging Gorman on. "Money'd have a blood color to it. Keep haunting me. Nope, expect we'd better keep on going."

"You're a fool!" Gorman screamed. "A pure, damned fool!"

"Maybe — to your way of thinking. But I figure the boot's on the other foot. You're the fool. You and your pa and your brothers."

Dan glanced ahead. "Marfa . . ." he called. "Pull up when we reach that butte. We'll hole up until daylight."

It would be better, he knew, if they could avoid a stop, but the horses needed rest, and Marfa could not go on much farther. Several times she had almost fallen from her saddle.

They pulled into the small, narrow clearing below the bluff and halted. Dan dismounted, stepped to the girl's side, and helped her off the buckskin. She smiled up at him.

"I'll get you something to eat," she murmured. "I don't want anything for myself. I'm — I'm too tired, I guess."

"Forget it then," Ricker said, pulling Burke's blanket roll free for her. "Fix yourself a bed and get some sleep. If I want anything, I'll get it."

As she turned away gratefully, he swung back to Gorman. The outlaw was still on his saddle, anger working at his lips. Dan felt his own temper rise.

"You heard me. We're spending the night here."

Stubbornly, the outlaw held his place. Ricker, abruptly furious, stepped forward. He seized Gorman by the arm, dragged him off the saddle, sent him sprawling onto the sand. Gorman rolled over and scrambled to his feet, his face livid.

"Damn you — you could've busted my leg . . ."

"Been all right with me," Ricker snapped. "You don't count — it's that horse you're riding I'm looking out for. Sit down there on that rock and keep your mouth shut."

He was not too concerned over the sorrel or the buckskin Marfa was riding. The red had watered and fed at Doherty's, and Burke's horse had received some care. But the black was a different matter. Jack had crowded him cruelly when he made his break, and the black was all but done for.

Ricker loosened the black's cinch and led him to a patch of thin grass. Taking Burke's canteen, he poured a little water on a rag and squeezed it dry into the suffering animal's mouth. The gelding gulped anxiously and strained for more. Dan repeated the process, then did what he could to slake the thirst of the sorrel and the buckskin. When he was finished the canteen was half empty. He glanced to Marfa, wondering if she needed a drink. She was already asleep. He took a small swallow himself, offered the container to Gorman who shook his head.

Shrugging, Dan hung the canteen back on Marfa's saddle and put the buckskin and sorrel out to graze with the black. He paused there when his eyes touched the saddlebags on his horse. He turned to Gorman.

"Want something to eat?"

He wasn't hungry himself, but he was not sure whether Gorman had taken food at Doherty's. The outlaw shook his head, leaned back against the surface of the butte.

"Nope. I'll be having myself a real breakfast before long. Steak and potatoes and eggs — along with some good black coffee. I'll be enjoying all that, Ricker, while you're eating dirt."

Dan pulled the rifle from Burke's saddle boot. "Don't bank on it," he said, and moved back into the center of the small clearing.

"You show some sense, and you and the girl can be sitting at that table with me."

"We'll wait until we reach Canyon City. Now you'd better be getting some sleep. Be a long day — and I don't figure on letting you hold me back."

"I ain't worried about it," Gorman said lightly. "Pa and the boys'll be here by daylight."

Ricker moved to the crest of a small hill a few yards to the south. He had nothing with which to tie up the outlaw, but he doubted if Jack would attempt an escape. There was no rock or stump available, so he settled down on the now cooling sand, laying the rifle across his knees.

He was tired and his eyes were heavy, but he knew he could not afford to sleep. Reaching for tobacco and papers, he rolled himself a smoke.

Jack Gorman was probably right. His kin would be near by daylight. The decoy camp would slow them some but not for long, and with fresh horses they would be able to close the gap swiftly. He glanced at Gorman. The outlaw was slumped against the face of the bluff, chin sunk into his chest. He was already dozing, apparently unworried, as he had maintained. Beyond him Marfa slept the sleep of the exhausted.

Dan puffed the cigarette down to a short stub, pinched out the coal, and flipped it away. His face felt stiff. He rubbed it briskly, dug out his makings, and spun up another slim cylinder. It was going to be a long night.

# CHAPTER
# THIRTEEN

At the faint crunch of sand Dan Ricker was instantly awake.

He came to his feet in a single bound, the rifle ready in his hands, inwardly cursing himself for falling asleep. His taut nerves relaxed. Standing before him was Marfa Talbot. In her hands was a sandwich of the now-stale bread and dried meat.

She smiled apologetically. "I thought you were awake."

"Should have been," he grumbled. He threw a glance at the camp. Jack Gorman still slept. Crooking the rifle in his arm, he took the sandwich, shifted his eyes to the east. Faint streaks of gray were beginning to show.

"How long've you been up?" he asked, turning back to her. She appeared rested. The few hours' sleep had done her much good.

"Just a short while. Would you like some water to go with that?"

"I'll get it later," he said. "Obliged to you for bringing my — my breakfast."

They both smiled at that. He came around and gave the hills and flats a swift scanning. The land was still indistinct with night's shadows, but he could see no riders.

"Guess we've been lucky," he said. "Gorman's bunch must have lost our trail and had to wait on daylight." He wolfed the rest of the bread and meat. "No use pushing it, though. Sooner we get moving, the better."

They returned to the camp. Dan roused Gorman, and while the outlaw ate the sandwich prepared for him by Marfa, he made ready the horses. The black was still in poor condition, but with careful handling he could make it through the day. Marfa's buckskin and his own sorrel were greatly improved.

A quarter hour later they were in the saddle and pulling away from the butte. Gorman, morose and silent, rode with his head down. Not until the sun had come out, warming the broad mesa over which they were passing, did he seem to become fully awake.

"Just about time for Pa and my brothers to be showing up," he said, yawning and glancing over his shoulder. "Sure be glad when they get here. Mighty tired of this saddle."

Dan made no comment. Marfa, riding at Gorman's left, favored the outlaw with a humorless look. He grinned back at her.

"You don't think they're coming? Well, I'll tell you for sure you can bet on it. And when they do, all this foolishness'll end, and we can head back to the ranch."

Gorman paused and studied the girl for a moment. "Just had me an idea. Why don't you come live at the ranch with us? You've got no folks now, no place to go. You could sort of do the housekeeping for us, look after things. Woman around the Double Diamond would be real handy. How about it?"

Without turning, Marfa shook her head. "Thank you, but I wouldn't be interested."

"Why not? Like I said, you've got no home, nobody. Or are you thinking you're too good to be doing housekeeping?"

She looked at him then, her gaze straight and cool. "I wouldn't mind that. It's the extra things you'd be expecting of me that I wouldn't care for."

Jack laughed, appearing surprised. "Extra things? Now, what would you be meaning by that?"

"You know what she's talking about," Ricker broke in harshly, secretly pleased at Marfa's firm refusal. "And she's right. Now forget it."

He twisted about and made a quick probe of the trail behind them. He stiffened. To that moment the horizon had been empty. Now four riders had appeared and were halted on the crest of a distant ridge.

"Pull up!" he barked, and drew the sorrel to a halt.

Swinging about, he shaded his eyes and squinted across the flat. It wasn't the Comancheros. There were too few — only four. One was a big man on a white horse. Undoubtedly Frank Gorman. He recognized a second — Clint Sandusky. The remaining pair would be Amos and Yancey, Jack's brothers.

"That's them," the outlaw said, a note of triumph in his voice. "That's Pa on his big white stud. Told you they'd be coming."

"Haven't caught us yet," Dan said. "Move out."

Jack did not stir. "Deal I offered you still goes. All we have to do is wait. When they get here, let me do the talking."

"You heard me — get going!" Ricker said savagely, and, spurring in close to the black, slapped him hard on the rump. Startled, the gelding spurted away for a dozen paces, then settled back to a walk.

"Keep that horse to a trot!" Dan shouted, riding in behind Gorman. Marfa was already setting a pace. "Keep up with the girl!"

Ricker looked ahead. There was no possible chance of outrunning the Gormans. None of their horses was up to it. There appeared to be no wooded area or rough badlands into which they could ride and find refuge; before them stretched only the endless plain, its level broken slightly here and there by short hills.

"You ain't got a prayer!" the outlaw yelled, his teeth showing in a sneering grin. "Better be listening to what I'm offering you."

Dan was only half-listening, giving no consideration at all to the proposition. He was planning ahead, struggling to shape his moves. He would have to send Marfa on, get her away from the point of trouble. He could not involve her in the gunplay that was bound to come.

He cast another glance over his shoulder. The Gormans had shortened the distance but were still far to the rear. Dan raised himself in his stirrups, probing the surrounding country again for a place where he could make a stand. There was nothing, not even brush clumps of a size sufficient to be of use. He settled back. Features grim, he angled to Marfa's side.

"The rifle — give it to me!" he shouted above the steady drum of the horses' hooves.

White-faced, she pulled the long gun from its boot and passed it to him.

"When they get close, I'll swing off," he said. "You keep riding. Don't want you near when the shooting starts."

She bit at her lips and shook her head. "I want to stay."

"No! Better if you're not around!" he said, and swung off behind Gorman.

He wouldn't be able to put up much of a fight, he knew. Out on the open, trapped, the Gormans would move in on him from all sides. But they wouldn't get off without paying a price; he'd see to that.

Suddenly hope began to move through him. Ahead on the horizon a shadow had materialized. He leaned forward and studied it intently. It was a house, a building of some kind. Larger shadow lay behind it — trees. Ricker continued to stare. Smaller structures became apparent. A homesteader!

Hope, in full-blown form, surged over Ricker. The place offered safety — salvation — the opportunity to hole up with his prisoner even if no physical assistance from the homesteader himself was forthcoming. And it meant Marfa would not be endangered. He grinned tightly. At least he now had a chance. He shouted at Marfa, pointing to the structures. She nodded and leaned lower over the buckskin.

Dan crowded up close to Gorman. "Put the spurs to your horse!" he ordered. "We're going to reach that house!"

Gorman scowled and squinted at the dwelling. "Like hell I will!" he shot back.

A tight-lipped smile cracked Ricker's mouth. He drew his pistol and took aim at Gorman. "A bullet in your shoulder make you change your mind?"

Jack blinked and swallowed hard. He dug his heels into the gelding's flanks. The black broke into a tired lope.

The structures grew in detail. The largest was low and squat, made of adobe bricks and wood. There was a corral behind it, along with smaller sheds and a barn. A figure — an old man, judging from the way he walked — was crossing the yard, a bucket in his hand.

Dan swiveled and checked on their pursuers. The Gormans had sighted the homesteader's place and quickened their pace. Ricker's jaw clamped shut. It would be close — a toss-up whether they could reach the house before the Gormans pulled into rifle range.

And it was questionable whether Jack's horse would make it at all.

Even the sorrel and the buckskin were having trouble maintaining the sprint. Ricker gauged the black's strength through critical eyes. He dropped back a few more yards. If the gelding faded and went down, he would have to move in fast, pick up Gorman, and rush on. There would be no moments to spare. Then it would be up to the big sorrel. Maybe there would be enough in him to carry double.

He crouched low, looking over the straining sorrel's head. The homesteader's place was no more than a quarter mile distant. The man in the yard had seen them, was now standing near the door watching them approach. If he saw the four riders farther to the rear he made no sign. It was possible he didn't; they were below a rise and lost even to Ricker's view at that moment.

Dan watched him set the bucket down, open the door, and enter the house. Ricker swore softly, hoping the homesteader would not become frightened and barricade his home. Their one real chance for safety lay inside, with the thick mud-brick walls between them and the Gormans.

They gained the edge of the clearing, started across the final, brief expanse of ground. Marfa was well ahead, her buckskin running strong. Suddenly Gorman's black stumbled and went to his knees in a boil of dust. Jack pitched over the exhausted animal's head, landing on all fours. Without hesitation, Ricker left the saddle in a long dive. He hit the ground just behind Gorman and bounded to his feet.

"Get up!" he shouted. "Get up and run, Goddamn you, or I'll blow your head off!"

Jack struggled to an upright position and attempted to dodge. Ricker lashed at him with his pistol. The barrel caught the outlaw on the cheekbone and laid a short gash in the skin. Gorman yelled, reversed his steps, and raced for the house.

Hard at his heels, Ricker glanced over his shoulder. The Gormans were no more than two hundred yards

**103**

away and coming fast. The sorrel trotted by, heading for the corral at the rear of the building. The black, again on his feet and limping badly, followed. Dan looked hurriedly around for Marfa. He grinned. She was off the buckskin and standing at the door, holding it open.

"Inside!" he yelled at Gorman as they thundered across the board stoop, and not waiting to let the outlaw hesitate, he shoved him through the entrance, paused long enough to let Marfa follow, and then crowded in behind her.

# CHAPTER
# FOURTEEN

"Drop the bar!" Dan shouted at Marfa, and rushed toward the rear of the house.

He burst into the adjoining room, the kitchen. The homesteader and his woman stood in the center of the area, their mouths agape, fear in their eyes. Ricker lunged by them, slammed the back door shut, secured it. Outside he heard the sharp pound of horses' hooves in the yard. They had barely made it.

Heaving for breath, Dan Ricker wheeled slowly and walked to where he had left Marfa and his prisoner. Gorman lay half-on, half-off a blanket-covered cot where he had fallen. He was gulping for wind. Marfa leaned against the wall. Her eyes were wide with excitement and the harsh strain of the past minutes. Her breast rose and fell rapidly as she too fought to recover from the hurried run. Ricker gave her a taut grin and wheeled to a window.

A vicious rattle of gunshots halted him midway. Bullets thudded into the thick walls of the house. There was a sound at the inner door. The homesteader, an old man with thin white hair, came into the room. His wife, much younger, crowded by him. She faced Ricker, anger lifting her color.

"Who are you? What do you want?"

There was another burst of gunfire. Dan grinned wryly. "Expect that answers your question."

The woman frowned, staring at Burke's badge pinned to his shirt. "You're — you're a lawman. And that man is your prisoner. Who are those men outside?"

"His kin. They're trying to get him away from me."

Jack Gorman pulled himself to his feet. He pointed at Ricker. "He's a damn liar — he's no lawman. Badge don't belong to him."

The homesteader came to life. "If you ain't no lawman," he said haltingly to Ricker, "then why — ?"

"Name's Dan Ricker. This man is a convicted murderer, and I'm trying to get him to Canyon City. He's been sentenced to hang."

"But if you ain't a lawman —"

"He murdered the lawman who was bringing him in. I happened to be there. Took it on myself to finish the job for him."

"And who's she?" the homesteader's woman said, nodding to Marfa. "Your wife?"

"No. She's riding with us — to Canyon City."

The woman's features darkened. "I see," she said coldly.

"I'm afraid you don't," Marfa broke in crisply. "And when we get time I'll explain it to you." She turned to Dan. "Is there anything you'd like me to do?"

Ricker shook his head. "Nothing. All we can do now is wait."

"You'll not wait here!" the homesteader's wife snapped, and stepped to the door. "This is our house — our home. You can't turn it into a fort!"

She gripped the drop bar and started to lift it from its thick wooden brackets. Ricker leaped across the room, jammed the length of oak back into place.

There was another splatter of bullets against the wall. Somewhere glass shattered. A deep voice shouted, "Ricker! You hear me in there, Ricker?"

The homesteader shuffled into the center of the room. He peered questioningly at Dan. "Then you ain't no real law?"

"He's nothing," Jack Gorman said, wiping at the blood smear on his cheek where Ricker's gunsight had slashed him. "Nothing but a saddlebum. That's all."

Dan swung to the outlaw, temper flaring. Gorman fell back a step. Ricker caught himself, shrugged. He faced the homesteader.

"Sorry I've had to do this, Mr . . ."

"Coyle — Rufus Coyle. And she's my wife, Esther."

"Mr. Coyle," Dan finished. "But they didn't give me much choice. Nothing will happen to you if we just sit tight. Soon as it's dark, I'll take my prisoner and slip out."

Coyle glanced at his wife. "Don't see no harm in that."

Mrs. Coyle sniffed. She glanced at Marfa. "What about her? She going too?"

"Was hoping you'd let her stay. I'll come back later for her — after I've turned my prisoner over to the authorities in Canyon City."

"And if you don't get back?"

"He'll come back," Marfa said quietly. "But if he doesn't, I'll go on by myself. I won't give you any trouble."

"Ricker! Listen to me!" Frank Gorman's heavy voice sounded again from the yard.

Jack laughed. "You're all just talking for nothing. Pa won't budge till he gets me out of here — and he'll tear this shack to pieces to do it, if he has to."

Dan moved to the window and glanced out. Frank Gorman, a large, powerfully built, graying man with a ramrod-straight backbone, was directly opposite the door. The white stallion he rode was dancing nervously about, throwing his head, jerking at the reins. To his left was a smaller edition of himself. That would be Amos, Ricker guessed.

The younger, darker man would be Yancey. He resembled Jack closely, seemed not too interested in what was taking place. Clint Sandusky, his left forearm wrapped in a crude bandage, waited a little apart.

"Ricker — I'm talking to you!"

"I hear," Dan replied.

"This is Frank Gorman. You get that? *Frank Gorman!*"

The big rancher must have been at the top of Ben Burke's list of kings, Dan thought.

"That supposed to mean something special to me?" he called back.

"It better. I've come after my son. Turn him loose."

"Not a chance."

"Then I'll come in there after him!"

Dan felt a hand on his shoulder. He turned. It was Rufus Coyle. His seamed face was pulled into deep worry, and his eyes were bright with concern.

"Them the Gormans out there?"

Ricker nodded. Coyle seemed to wilt. He turned to his wife. Esther Coyle had blanched, and her lips were quivering.

"It's the Gormans," Coyle mumbled. "The Gormans. They'll burn us out — tear the place down sure."

For a moment there was only the sound of Jack's quiet laughing. Then from the yard came his father's voice, strong and harsh.

"You've got five minutes! Five minutes — hear? Then I'm taking my boy, one way or another."

"Don't worry," Marfa said, moving to the side of the older woman. "Long as we're inside they can't hurt us."

"But they can wreck everything outside," Esther Coyle said, beginning to sob. "They can burn the barn and the sheds — kill the livestock . . . We don't have much, but it means a lot to us."

She pulled away abruptly and moved slowly to the kitchen. Rufus Coyle followed. They began to speak, their words low and indistinguishable.

"Better listen to Pa," Jack Gorman warned. "He'll do what the old woman said, sure as hell."

Ricker shook his head and stood for a few moments in the dead center of the room listening to the murmuring in the kitchen.

"Time's about up, Ricker!"

Dan walked to the window and threw his glance into the yard. Perhaps he could slip Jack out the back door and make a run for the barn without Gorman and his party noticing. Such would relieve the situation. And any shooting would be better done from that point.

The idea died in his mind. It was too late. Frank Gorman was alone. Yancey had moved off to cover the north side of the house. Sandusky was to the south. That meant Amos now stood guard at the rear.

"What's it goin' to be, Ricker?"

Dan heard the cot scrape as Jack Gorman lunged by it on his way to the window.

"You'll have to come in, Pa! He ain't turning me loose!"

Ricker took two long steps forward. His fist shot out, caught the outlaw on the jaw, knocked him back onto the cot.

"Stay there!" he snarled. He whirled to Marfa. "Get down low, and keep down. Don't know just what happens next, but —"

"I know!" Rufus Coyle shouted from the kitchen. "I ain't lettin' them burn down my place!"

Dan spun. He saw the homesteader lunge toward the back door, saw him grasp the crossbar that secured it and throw it aside. The thick panel swung inward. Amos Gorman, gun in hand, rushed through the opening.

# CHAPTER
# FIFTEEN

Ricker's weapon came up smooth and fast. He dropped to a crouch, prepared to meet the charging Amos. Caution stayed his trigger finger. Rufus Coyle was in the line of fire. And there were Esther Coyle and Marfa to consider.

He wheeled away from the inner doorway, knowing Amos would entertain no such thoughts; he would instead take advantage of it. He heard Marfa scream his name, and he pivoted. Jack Gorman was lunging at him, hopeful of overpowering him and carrying him to the floor.

Dan sidestepped the outlaw's rush. He reached out, caught Jack by the arm, spun him about. With all the strength he could muster, he hurled Gorman straight into the oncoming Amos.

The impact of the collision set dishes to rattling in the kitchen. Amos went down hard, and Jack ricocheted into the nearby wall, overturning a small table and jarring a picture to the floor. Outside, Dan could hear Frank Gorman shouting questions, demanding to know what was going on. Evidently he and the others did not know that Amos, bent on claiming glory for himself, had gained entry to the house. But they would soon learn and come storming in.

"Get out of here!" Dan yelled hoarsely at Marfa. "There'll be shooting!"

The girl stared across the room, heading for the kitchen. Amos, half-up, made a frantic grab for her. She pulled back and came up against Ricker. Dan caught her with his left arm and prevented her from falling. Immediately, he pushed her toward another inner door, one that apparently led to bedrooms.

"In there — hurry!"

As he wheeled, his foot came up against an overturned chair. He started to kick it aside, thought better of it. Grasping it by the top, he lifted it from the floor and threw it at Amos Gorman. Amos yelled, tried to dodge, failed. The rocker struck him on the chest and head. He went down again, losing his gun.

Dan leaped for the weapon. He kicked and sent the heavy sixgun skittering across the floor out of reach. Intuition brought him around fast. Jack was surging in from the left, his still-bound wrists upraised like a club. He tried to jerk away as Marfa screamed, but he was too late. Jack's locked hands thudded against the side of his head with the force of a hammer. Lights popped before his eyes and he felt himself falling. Vaguely, he could hear Frank Gorman's voice.

"Ricker! Ricker! Time's up . . ."

He went to his hands and knees, senses swimming in an ocean of mist. Immediately in front of him Amos was pulling himself groggily to his feet, shaking his head like some huge, wounded beast.

Dan gasped as something smashed into his ribcage and drove the breath from him. Jack — he had forgotten momentarily that the killer was standing over him. Gorman kicked him again, sent pain roaring through his body.

Ricker threw himself to one side. Jack was cursing steadily, wildly, striking out with his feet. Dan managed to dodge the next blow. He caught at Gorman's boot and jerked hard. Jack went off-balance and staggered back into the wall once more.

Ricker, his wits assembling fast, rolled over and bounded to an upright position. He rushed toward Amos, who was now standing, legs spread, eyes still glazed from the encounter with the chair. Doubling his fist, Dan smashed a hard right to the man's jaw. Amos spun half-about from the blow. His arms dropped to his sides as his head snapped back. He took a short half step backward and collapsed silently.

"Ricker — we're comin' in!"

Dan threw a quick glance at Marfa. She was standing against the far wall. He gave her a taut, reassuring grin and strode to where Jack Gorman, still slightly dazed, sagged against the wall. He grasped the killer by the arm and pushed him toward the kitchen and its outside door.

"Move!" he gritted, jamming his gun barrel into the man's spine. "Do what I tell you or I'll blow you in two."

"What . . . ?" Gorman mumbled, holding back.

Dan gouged him savagely. "When we get to the door, make a run for the horses."

"You'll — you'll never make it!" the killer cried. "They'll cut you down before —"

"Then I'll take you with me. You better yell and tell your pa that if they try!"

They reached the doorway and broke out into the yard. "You're a damn fool!" Jack complained bitterly. "All this hullabaloo, and it don't mean nothing to you! You ain't even a lawman!"

"Means plenty to me now," Ricker answered as they started across the open ground. "Run!"

They reached the horses. Gorman had trouble pulling himself onto the saddle, but under the heartless prodding of Ricker's gun, he managed. Dan leaped onto the sorrel and whirled about. A small patch of trees and brush stood a short distance beyond the barn. He pointed toward them.

"That's where we're —"

A yell went up from the yard. It was Sandusky's voice.

"There they go — out back!"

There was a sudden hammer of hooves as Frank Gorman, followed by the others, came thundering around the house. Dan wheeled in close to Jack. He put his pistol to the killer's head.

"Sing out! Tell them to hold it!"

Jack took one look at Ricker's frozen, desperate face. "Pa!" he screamed. "Wait! Don't try anything. He'll shoot — I know he will!"

Frank Gorman, trailed closely by Clint Sandusky and Yancey, came to a sliding halt at the rear of the Coyle house.

114

"He means it, Pa!" Jack shouted. "He's plumb *loco!*"

The elder Gorman said something to Sandusky. The tall rider dropped from his saddle and entered the building. The rancher then swung his hard-cornered visage to Dan.

"What's next, mister? What's the deal?"

"I'm taking Jack to Canyon City, dead or alive," Ricker replied. "Might as well get that in your head. Makes no difference to me which way. And if you try to stop me, he'll still end up full of lead."

"No need to be talking like that," Gorman said. "Seems to me we ought to be able to work this out."

Dan shook his head. "I'm taking him in."

Gorman glanced at the doorway. He pulled off his hat and scratched at his thatch of iron-gray hair.

"Why? What's got you so fired up over Jack? He never did anything to you. And you ain't no lawman."

Ricker sighed. "No use trying to explain. Man like you'd never understand."

"Maybe I wouldn't," the rancher said, shrugging. "But it makes no difference. Point is, that's my boy there you're cartin' off to get hung. You know damn well I can't allow that."

"Why can't you? He's a killer. He's no different from any murderer. He's got to hang like any man that's been convicted and sentenced for a killing."

"That's what you think. I figure it otherwise. I don't aim to let anybody hang a son of mine." There was a fierceness to Gorman's declaration, a determination that recognized no obstacles.

"About time you were learning you're not bigger than the law," Dan said wearily. "You can't do as you please, Gorman. Not any more. This country's changed."

"Nothing's changed in my part of Texas. I'm still top dog around here — and you sure better believe it!"

Ricker shifted on his saddle. "Like I said, talking sense to you is a waste of time. Now — do I ride out of here with my prisoner, or do we settle it with guns? Either way, you've got a dead man for a son."

Gorman pulled on his hat. "I figure to make a bargain with you —"

"No bargains!" Dan snapped. "You heard my terms."

The rancher stepped down from his horse. He cocked his head to one side. "Your terms," he echoed. "Well, here's mine."

He half-turned to the doorway. Dan saw movement in the shadowy interior of the room, and then Amos and Clint Sandusky appeared. They held Marfa Talbot between them.

# CHAPTER
# SIXTEEN

The girl was struggling frantically to free herself but with no success. The two men had her in a tight grip, one to each arm. As they came into the yard Rufus Coyle, apparently now repenting his rash action, followed.

He threw himself upon Sandusky and fought to loosen the puncher's fingers. Frank Gorman stepped up and dealt the aged homesteader a hard, back-handed blow to the head. The man dropped into a dusty heap. Esther Coyle screamed, her cry a shrill sound in the afternoon's hush. She bolted through the doorway and dropped upon her husband.

Frank Gorman watched for a moment, then lifted his flat gaze to Dan. A crooked smile was on his lips as he hooked his thumbs in his belt.

"See how it is, friend? These are my terms — turn Jack loose or I take it out on the sodbusters."

Anger was a seething force within Ricker. In a barely controlled voice he said, "You're a brave man, Gorman."

"Being brave's got nothing to do with it. Happens I know how to get things my way."

"Don't listen to him, Dan," Marfa said unexpectedly. "Go on — take your prisoner out of here. He won't dare harm us."

Gorman swung his sardonic eyes to the girl. "What makes you think so, sister? What's a couple of sodbusters less in this country? Be doing it a favor."

"You wouldn't kill us," Marfa said stiffly, standing up to the rancher. "You wouldn't risk that."

Gorman shrugged and spat contemptuously. "Don't fool yourself. But that ain't exactly what I had in mind. Show her, Clint."

Grinning, Sandusky grasped the collar of Marfa's shirt with his free hand. With a downward sweep he ripped the garment from her. She cried out and clung to the shredded cloth by pressing it to her body with her elbows. Laughing, Clint jerked it free and tossed it to the ground.

"That's a start," Frank Gorman said. "Ain't sure what we'll find under them fancy lace doodads. Something mighty interesting, I expect. Up to you, Ricker, whether we find out."

The anger within Dan heightened — anger and a strong disgust. "Should have figured you for that kind of a man — seeing how your son turned out."

"Jack? Oh, I reckon he's a splinter off the old stump, sure enough. But that ain't here nor there. Question is — what're you going to do?"

"I expected to be up against a real man."

"I'm more man than you'll ever bump into, Ricker, even if you live a hundred years — which you ain't likely to do. I just got the knack of getting things done."

"By shaming a girl."

"Hell, you ain't seen half what I've got figured out for her if you don't come to terms. It's this way — if you don't come to terms, you think I'll go chasing after you? Not much. That'd be plain dumb. I plan for me and the boys to just move in with the sodbusters and let the girl look after us. She'll be a right pretty sight, walking around here jaybird naked, doing her chores . . ."

A strangled oath slipped through Ricker's lips. He stirred angrily.

"You want to know why we won't go trailin' after you, Ricker? Because I know your kind. You'd keep thinking about the girl, worrying over it. And before long it'd get to you and you'd turn right around and hightail it back here. You'd beg me to take Jack off your hands. I'm telling you straight, ain't I, Ricker?"

Dan's eyes were on Marfa. She had lapsed into a shocked silence as she contemplated the possibilities that lay before her. And he knew she was wondering what was in his mind — what decision he would make. Her bare shoulders, pale ivory in the yellowing sunlight, trembled visibly.

At that moment Rufus Coyle struggled to sit up. His wife aided him tenderly. The homesteader rubbed at his head and looked around absently, dazed and hurt. Sandusky raised his leg, placed his foot against the old man's shoulder, sent him sprawling.

"Reckon the old folks'll just be in the way," Gorman continued, his eyes on the writhing figure in the dust. "They'd just have to disappear. Wouldn't want to be

**119**

listening to their bleatin'." The rancher paused and focused his attention on Dan. "Well, Mr. Ricker, what's it going to be? I'm a mite tired of jawing."

Dan knew he had no choice, but in those fleeting moments he cast about in his mind frantically for another answer to his problem. He could not leave Marfa and the Coyles to the barbarities of the Gormans and Clint Sandusky; such was unthinkable. But to hand over Jack galled him. The outlaw was a coldblooded killer, deserved his fate — and should be led to it regardless of all else.

But should it matter so deeply to him? He was no sworn lawman — only one by proxy. Why not let Jack go? He would run afoul of the law again, likely soon, and it would become the responsibility of another marshal, like Ben Burke, to settle the matter. Sure . . . turn him loose to kill someone else. Dan groaned. And freeing him would have even further meaning; it would strengthen the belief that men such as Frank Gorman were invincible — that they were indeed kings in their own right.

He thought of Yancey Gorman. Burke had said he was the best of the lot. So far he had taken no part in either the proceedings or the conversation. He simply sat his small, black horse and watched. Dan turned his burning glance to him.

"Where do you stand on this, mister? Been told you're a cut above the others. You go along with your pa?"

"You're damn right he does!" Frank Gorman roared, abruptly aroused. "He does what I tell him."

**120**

"I'm asking him," Ricker said coolly. "What about it, Yancey?"

The middle son of the Gorman clan returned Ricker's pushing gaze without blinking. After a long minute he shrugged. "Pa's doings. He's running things."

Dan's hopes collapsed. "And you've got nothing to say about it," he said heavily. "You're not man enough to speak out against something you know's wrong."

Yancey shifted restlessly. "I ain't saying nothing."

Frank Gorman's lips pulled into a sneer. "Guess you see who bosses my outfit. You satisfied?"

Dan made no reply. Yancey had been his last, solitary chance, and it had not panned out.

"Come on — I'm tired of waiting," Gorman said, wheeling about. He motioned to Sandusky. "Start stripping her, Clint. Let's get this show going."

"Hold it!" Ricker yelled as Marfa began to struggle.

Gorman lifted his broad hand to halt the puncher's eager motions. "Yeah?"

"You win," Dan said, lowering his gun. "I'll turn him loose. Let the girl go. I'm taking you at your word that you'll ride out without harming her or the others."

Gorman smiled. "You got my word," he said softly. "You sure have. Now, bring Jack over here to me."

# CHAPTER
# SEVENTEEN

"Turn the girl loose," Dan said again, not moving.

Gorman nodded his head at Amos and Sandusky. They released their hold on Marfa's arms. She jerked away, bent down and swiftly gathered the remnants of her shirt, then moved to the side of Rufus Coyle and helped him to rise.

"All right," Gorman said. "Come on."

Dan dropped his pistol into its holster. Jack touched his horse with spurs and guided it toward the rancher and the others. Ricker followed slowly, warily. Marfa and Mrs. Coyle had finally got Rufus to his feet and were helping him into the house. The door closed behind them, and Dan heard the crossbar drop into place. A sigh slipped from his lips. They were out of it now.

Jack Gorman came off the gelding hurriedly, almost falling in his haste. He held his bound wrists out for Clint Sandusky to cut the rope. His father shook his head.

"Ricker tied him up. Ricker can get down and turn him loose."

Dan, still on his sorrel and thoroughly suspicious, said, "Clint can do it."

Gorman whipped out his gun and leveled it at Ricker. "Get off that horse, you saddlebum!" he snarled.

Dan hesitated briefly and swung down. His face was taut, angry, and a long shrill warning of what was to come raced through him. He remained motionless, making no move to help Jack.

"His gun, Amos," Frank Gorman murmured. "Get it."

The eldest brother stepped to Dan's side, plucked the weapon from its leather case, and tossed it off toward the corral.

"Untie him," the rancher said again.

Jack turned about, extended his hands to Ricker. There was a broad smirk on the killer's face, and a wild, dancing light filled his eyes.

"You heard Pa, you fake tinhorn lawman! Get 'em off me!"

Dan pulled the knot apart, let the length of rope drop to the ground. The yard was in silence as the rest of the Gorman party waited expectantly.

Jack rubbed at his wrists. Dan eyed the man narrowly, ready for anything. It came suddenly. Jack swung a hard, roundhouse right at Ricker's head. Dan avoided the awkward blow, countered with a straight left and quick right that drove Jack to his knees.

Amos Gorman shouted a curse and lunged. Dan wheeled, rocked him to his heels with a stiff blow to the face, but before he could spin again, Clint Sandusky was swarming in, catching him by the arms and pinning them to his sides. He tried to wrestle free, but Jack

Gorman was up, coming at him from the left. He took a shocking blow to the belly and doubled half-over. Sandusky pulled him upright.

Gasping for wind, supported by Sandusky, Dan glared at Frank Gorman, who, with gun still in his hand, was watching it all with an expressionless face.

"You're — you're . . . a man . . . of your . . . word, Gorman."

The rancher shrugged. "Was talking about the sodbusters. Didn't say nothin' about you. Work him over good, boys."

Immediately Jack sank his fist into Ricker's belly again and followed with a smash to the chin that brought Dan's head up sharply.

"Let me in on this!" Amos Gorman shouted, and crowding his younger brother aside, he rushed in with both arms swinging.

Pain shot through Dan Ricker in a succession of jagged waves, and then a numbness set in, mercifully blotting out all sensation. Like a rag doll he was buffeted and hammered from one man to another, never being permitted to fall, but tossed back and forth on rubbery legs.

"Got me a few good licks comin' too."

Vaguely, as if from a great distance, Dan heard Clint Sandusky's voice. Through a hazy fog he saw the puncher's grinning face before him, watched in a sort of suspended fascination as the rider smashed at him, rocked him from side to side, but evoked no feeling of pain.

"He's had enough, Pa."

It was Yancey Gorman speaking. He could see the man's lips move, but the words seemed oddly detached.

Frank Gorman spat. "Want him taught a lesson. Want him to remember it ain't smart to buck a Gorman."

"They'll kill him if you don't call them off. He's out on his feet now. Don't even know they're beating him."

After a bit, the rancher nodded. "Guess you're right. Anyway, it's getting late. And we got us a long ride waiting."

The rancher walked into the churning knot of men and pushed them aside. "That'll do," he said.

Ricker, on his feet by sheer will, his eyes wide with shock, gazed at Gorman stupidly. The rancher seized him by his shirt front and jerked him erect.

"Get out of Texas — and stay out!" he said. "It's a dead end for you, cowboy!"

The words registered dully on Dan's brain. Gorman released his grasp, and he began to sink, his legs refusing to support him further.

"Go . . . to . . . hell!" he mumbled thickly.

Gorman lashed out angrily with his open hand. The blow caught Ricker on the ear. He went over backward into the dust.

# CHAPTER
# EIGHTEEN

Dan Ricker was conscious first of the throbbing pain and monotonous aching that possessed his body. Then he became aware that he was in a room and that it was night, for a lamp standing in the center of a small table nearby burned brightly. He was on a bed, soft and clean-smelling. And there was someone bending over him.

Marfa.

He looked up at her, straining to see through swollen, half-closed eyes. Her face was a pale, sweet oval in the soft golden light. She had a cloth in her hand, applying it to various parts of his head. There was some kind of medicine on the pad, for his skin smarted and stung when she touched him.

Darkness, soft and thick, claimed him again, and he slid off into a deep, pain-filled chasm where all things whirled and left him breathless and choking; a vast despair engulfed him. He seemed to have no strength and could do nothing to help himself. He could only spin on and on, endlessly.

When he opened his eyes the second time daylight was streaming through a lace-curtained window opposite the bed. He felt much better. The throbbing had subsided to a dull ache, and the stabbing pain had gone. He pulled himself to a sitting position, flinching as his muscles reacted to the effort. But he managed it.

He glanced about the small, meagerly furnished room and saw Marfa curled up in a chair near the door. She was sleeping. Evidently she had been up the entire night caring for him.

He studied her intently as though never really seeing her before. Her hair had come down and was now coiled about her head in thick swirls of palest gold. Her cheeks were a soft cream color, and back close to her neck the skin was white where the sun had failed to touch. She had a firm chin, and her nose was slightly uptilted. He had not noticed that before either — but, he thought wryly, there hadn't been time to notice much of anything.

He raised his arms, moved them, flexed his fingers experimentally. He shifted his legs. He had been lucky — he had no broken bones to show for the encounter. But his ribs were sore, and it hurt somewhat to breathe deeply. The Gormans must have really worked him over. He tried to remember, but the whole thing was vague.

The door opened slightly. Rufus Coyle's head appeared. A dark welt along the left side of his face marked the location of Frank Gorman's brutal blow. He stared at Ricker and smiled. Dan nodded, pointed to Marfa, and placed his fingers to his lips in a gesture for silence. The old man bobbed his head and withdrew, closing the door softly.

Dan sank back and allowed his eyes to make a slow tour of the room. His gaze halted on a small chest of drawers near the head of the bed. A hand mirror lay on its top. He reached for it and stared wonderingly at his own reflection.

Dark bluish swellings lay below his eyes. A lengthy red scratch extended from his left ear to the corner of his mouth. One of the Gormans, or Clint Sandusky, had been wearing a ring. His lips were puffed, and there was a cut in his chin. His face appeared slightly lopsided.

"You look like you walked into a mowing machine." Marfa's voice startled him.

He lowered the mirror almost in embarrassment and grinned at her. "For a fact. Mower probably would've done less damage."

"At least," she said, rising, "you're alive."

He nodded and looked about the room. "My duds? Got to get moving."

She paused on her way to the door. "I — I don't know if you should," she said doubtfully.

"Been in worse shape. My clothes?"

"Mrs. Coyle fixed them last night. They were in pretty bad condition. I'll get them."

She disappeared into the adjoining room. She returned a few moments later and laid his clothing on the bed. "Breakfast will be ready when you come out. Will you shave first?"

Dan explored the stubble that covered his cheeks gingerly and flinched. "Reckon I'll pass that up for a couple of days."

Marfa smiled and withdrew. Ricker swung about and threw his legs over the edge of the bed. His head swam briefly, and his muscles cried out in protest. He sat quietly for a time until the discomfort faded, and then he began to dress. It was a considerable effort, but eventually it was accomplished.

He rose and crossed the room, walking stiffly. He opened the door and entered the adjacent area. It was the front room, where, that day previous, the fighting had taken place. Everything was in order now, and there were no signs of any disturbance. He continued on to the kitchen. Marfa and the Coyles were seated at a table drinking coffee. The air was pleasant with the savory odors of bacon and fried potatoes.

Rufus got to his feet, apology on his weathered face. "Mr. Ricker," he began hurriedly, "got to explain about yesterday . . . about why I opened that there door, let in the Gormans . . ."

"Forget it," Dan said. "It's over and done with now."

"Can't. Got to tell you — make you see. I know about the Gormans. They're mean — real mean. Knew they would tear my place down if I didn't do what they said — maybe do somethin' bad to my wife and me. And the girl."

Dan, eyes on the floor, said nothing. There was no answer to what Coyle had said, and he couldn't find it in his heart to blame the old man. Against the Gormans the homesteader had no defense.

"You did what you figured you had to do," he said finally. "In your boots I'd likely have done the same. Don't think any more about it."

Coyle lowered his head in relief. "Obliged to you for seein' it that way. Reckon a man never gets too old to learn, however. Found out you still can't do business with the likes of the Gormans, no matter what you do. Now, set yourself down and have a bite to eat."

Dan lowered himself into a chair, gritting his teeth as pain slashed through his body. He brushed at the beads of sweat that popped out on his forehead and grinned.

"Expect I ought to be thanking you instead of you thanking me. Was kind of you to take me in, doctor me up. Hate to think what I'd feel like if you hadn't."

His eyes were on Marfa as he spoke. She met his gaze, smiled, turned to pour him a cup of coffee. Mrs. Coyle was at the black cast-iron stove heaping a plate with steaming food.

"Want to thank you, too, ma'am," he said to Esther Coyle, "for fixing up my clothes. They're not much, but they're all I've got."

"Wasn't anything," the elderly woman replied with no enthusiasm.

Ricker shrugged. That she disapproved of him, blamed him for the trouble that had befallen them, was evident. She was right, of course.

"I'll be riding on soon as I've eaten," he said as she set the plate before him. "Don't want to cause you any more grief."

Immediately Marfa frowned. "You're in no condition to travel. You ought to rest another day and night, at least."

Mrs. Coyle sniffed audibly and turned back to her stove. Rufus kept his eyes fastened upon the contents of his coffee cup.

"I'll do fine," Dan said, smiling at the girl. "You're a good doctor. After I move around a bit the stiffness will leave. Already feeling better."

He began to eat, slowly and with relish, enjoying each swallow of the delicious food. The first sip of coffee warmed him, loosened his muscles, seemed to give him new strength. He smiled again at Marfa.

"Meal like this will cure a man of anything."

Esther Coyle wheeled slowly about. "Just an ordinary breakfast. Have it every day. You talk like it's something special."

"It is for me," Ricker said. "Been a long time since I had a home — and ate meals like this."

There was silence for a time; then, in a small voice Marfa said, "Where will you go?"

He hesitated, stalled by the question. It had not occurred to him up to that moment, had hung back in his mind as though reluctant to be considered. Now it faced him squarely: finish the job he started out to do — or ride on?

He had no real reason to keep after Jack Gorman, to try again to bring him to justice; it was not his job. He was no lawman — and he had already done more than his part. All the good reasons for forgetting Gorman were there, but somehow the quiet, set features of Ben Burke kept crowding them aside, and the soft, drawling truths he had spoken continued to trickle through Dan's mind.

"If the Coyles don't mind your staying here for a spell, I'll go after Jack and take him on to Canyon City. Then I'll come for you."

"No!" The word burst from Marfa's lips unexpectedly. "You can't do it — they'll kill you this time!"

"She's right," Rufus Coyle said, rousing from his lethargy. "Gorman plain don't want you around here."

"Guess that's the reason I've got to do it," Dan said soberly. "Men like Frank Gorman've got to learn they can't highhand things to suit themselves. That, and the fact that Jack's an escaped killer."

"It's not up to you," Marfa said quietly. "It's a job for the law. The regular law."

Ricker shook his head. "You figure there's a sheriff or a marshal anywhere around here who'll go after Jack and arrest him?"

Marfa stared at him, then looked down. "No. I guess not. Everybody's afraid of the Gormans."

"Then you know why I've got to do it."

Marfa rose and moved to the window. "I suppose so. Only . . ."

"Only what?"

"It seems so foolhardy — and hopeless. Against the Gormans . . ."

"Not as bad as you think, and I never was much of a hand to take long chances."

"You can't avoid it, if you go after Jack."

"Man can use his head. Learned that when I was just a kid." Ricker paused. "Gives me a sort of warm feeling knowing you're worried about me. I'll be back. It's a promise."

132

She turned to face him. "I'll hold you to that promise," she said.

Rufus Coyle got up and went into the adjoining room. He returned shortly bringing Dan's pistol.

"Found it last night," the old man said, laying it on the table. "One of the Gormans kicked it over by the corral. I cleaned it up good and oiled it. Figured it ought to be looked after."

"Appreciate that," Dan said, slipping the weapon into its holster.

"Took care of your sorrel, too. He's been rubbed down good and fed. Was a mighty beat-lookin' critter. He's fine now."

"Another favor I owe you," Ricker said, pushing back from the table. He stood up and faced Esther Coyle.

"I won't insult you, ma'am, by offering to pay you for your hospitality, but I would like to buy a little grub for the trail. Meat, some coffee beans, a handful of those biscuits will do. And I need something I can carry water in."

"Got an extry canteen in the barn," Rufus broke in. "I'll fill it up and hang it on your saddle. Esther, you and Marfa get the victuals ready for him," he added, and headed out into the yard.

"I'll mind the victuals," Mrs. Coyle said, brushing by the girl. "You and him go on outside. Little walking will do him good."

Marfa took Dan by the hand and led him toward the door. Ricker hesitated beside Esther Coyle. "I'll say again I'm sorry for the trouble I caused you . . . And I thank you again for your hospitality, too."

**133**

She looked at him briefly, smiled, and resumed her chore of preparing his trail supplies.

Dan followed Marfa into the warm sunshine. Side by side they circled the house, strolled through the short rows of corn and by the vegetable garden, then slanted for the barn. The first few yards were pure agony for Ricker, but gradually the pains began to fade as his muscles regained their resiliency, and by the time they reached the building where Rufus worked with the sorrel, he was feeling considerably better.

Coyle saw them coming and led the big red horse out to meet them. As he handed the leathers to Dan, he said, "Horse of yours is ready for anythin'. Finer'n frog hair, in fact. You won't need to worry none about him." The old homesteader paused and extended his hand. "Best o' luck to you, son, and we'll be lookin' for you back. And don't fret about the lady here. We'll look after her."

Ricker nodded and took the man's fingers into his own. "I'll be back. So long."

Dan thrust his foot into the stirrup and swung to the saddle as Coyle shambled off toward the house. He smiled down at Marfa. "I meant that."

"And I'll be waiting," she said.

He leaned far over, over, ignoring the protest of his muscles, and kissed her lightly on the lips. "*Adiós*," he said, and put the sorrel into motion.

As he drew up alongside the house Rufus Coyle appeared and held out a flour sack well filled with food.

**134**

"Don't go offerin' to pay for that either," he said as Dan began to stow it in his saddlebags. "We ain't that kind of people."

Ricker grinned his thanks and straightened up. He stared out across the flat. "Which way to the Gorman place?"

"Straight east. Can't miss it," the homesteader said, and stepped back.

Dan moved on. When he reached the end of the yard he glanced over his shoulder. Marfa had not stirred. She raised her hand hesitantly, almost hopefully, as though she thought he might yet turn back.

Ricker touched the brim of his hat and rode on.

# CHAPTER
# NINETEEN

Straight east — and seven hours' steady riding.

Dan Ricker had not anticipated such a lengthy trip to the headquarters of Gorman's Double Diamond spread. But finally he was there.

He halted now on the rim of a high bluff that overlooked the long, somewhat narrow valley in which the ranch lay. A bright streak of silver cut its way along the center of the swale, and the land was green with trees and gently blowing grass.

The main house was a huge, rambling affair set a little apart from the dozen or so other structures that made up the place. The nearest to it was apparently the kitchen, judging from the smoke that twisted up from the chimney. The square building adjoining it would be the crew's quarters. Farther on stood a barn, a wagon shed, and various other structures. A maze of corrals lay to the east of the cluster. Some contained cattle; others, horses.

The ranch had an efficient, businesslike appearance. There was no wasted area; no flowers or similar womanly influence was visible. Frank Gorman's empire was devoted strictly to the raising and marketing of beef — and of that he had plenty.

**136**

Dan had swung wide of several herds that day, all wearing the twin diamond brand. He had been careful to avoid contact with any of Gorman's riders, not wishing to be halted and forced to explain his presence on the range. Once, he thought he had been seen and was being followed; five horsemen, somehow vaguely familiar, appeared in the distance. But before they were near enough to recognize, they dropped behind a ridge and were lost to view. He never saw them again.

He had no exact plan in mind. His method was simply to get close and hang around the fringe of the ranch until an opportunity presented itself or something happened that would enable him to recapture Jack. Simply to ride in and demand the outlaw was sheer folly, and he did not consider it. The Gormans would shoot him down before he could even get the words spoken.

Whatever he did, however, could not be done until darkness, so he dismounted, dropped back below the rim, and picketed the sorrel to a withered, weather-toughened old juniper tree. Then, moving again to the crest, he sprawled onto his belly to watch and await nightfall.

Riders came and went. Two wranglers, evidently working with the blacksmith at the chore of shoeing some of the riding stock, appeared periodically leading the horses to and from the corral. He saw Amos Gorman come from the main house and walk to the kitchen. There was no sign of the remainder of the family, although a pinto horse in the yard told him that Clint Sandusky was around somewhere. Jack's gelding was not to be seen, but he likely was inside the barn, resting.

As he looked down from the height, Dan fixed the layout of the ranch firmly in his mind. When it became night, he would descend from the butte and approach the house from the south side. Shades were all drawn over the windows in that wall; he assumed the bedrooms lay there. Not only would his chances for moving in unseen be better at that angle, but there was a strip of thick brush close to the house that would provide ideal cover for the sorrel.

He could not see the front of Gorman's, and he had no idea of what lay to the north. It could be a problem he might have to face later, but for the present he would concentrate on gaining the south wall.

The afternoon wore on. Yancey Gorman and four men rode in, left their horses in the corral, and separated. Yancey headed toward the main house while the riders angled for their quarters. Not long after that a figure emerged from the kitchen and began to beat an echoing tattoo on the iron triangle suspended from the corner of the building. Dan watched the man complete the summons and return to his kitchen.

Almost immediately Frank Gorman, accompanied by Yancey, appeared and strode purposefully across the yard, his huge figure a strong, powerful shape in the sunlight. Other men came from the bunkhouse and fell in alongside them.

Dan stirred, frowning. Jack had not shown himself yet. Could it be that the elder Gorman had sent him elsewhere — back to Mexico, perhaps? Ricker relaxed.

Jack, with Clint Sandusky in tow, came into the open and hurried for the dining quarters. Something had delayed him apparently, and he was now hastening to take his place at the table.

Feeling hunger himself, Dan pulled back to the sorrel. Taking the canteen and the sack of food the Coyles had provided, he returned to the crest. Gorman and his crew would be inside for a good half hour longer, he guessed, but he would take no chance on it. Jack might decide to leave.

Stretched out on the warm sand, with the sun sinking lower into a yellow blaze beyond the hills to the west, Ricker munched on the fried meat and biscuits Esther Coyle had placed in the sack. He dared not risk a fire for coffee, so he washed it all down with water. It was a filling meal, if not too satisfying, but Dan was accustomed to frugal fare and thought nothing of it.

It did turn his thoughts to Marfa Talbot, and he fell to wondering about her — remembering the way she looked, the soft curve of her face, the depth of her eyes and how they looked when he had kissed her. He continued to marvel at his earlier blindness where she was concerned, and the fact that they all were under extreme stress at the time seemed a poor reason. She was a woman any man would quickly notice — actually worth chucking the whole Jack Gorman affair for.

In the same thought he knew it would be the wrong thing to do. Not only was he conscience-bound to carry out his self-imposed duty, but he also realized that Marfa would want it that way. She might protest his exposing himself to danger — but she would not want him to take the easier course, either.

Should he do so she likely would say nothing to him, but it would always be there in her mind, just as it would be in his. And there would be no wiping it away for either of them. Like a malignant sore it would fester and grow until finally it became a solid influence affecting their lives.

He finished his eating and restored the sack and canteen to the saddle. Again he made his way to the rim of the bluff, his thoughts still revolving around Marfa and the future. As he settled down in the closing darkness, the kitchen door was flung open and men moved into the yard. Some walked on for the bunkhouse, weary and seeking rest after the day's hard labor. Others paused and leaned back against a convenient wall to enjoy a cigarette or pipe.

Frank Gorman, now with all his sons and Clint Sandusky, came out last of all. Together they walked to the barn and spent a lengthy ten minutes inside. They reappeared, sauntered to the main house, and were again lost to Ricker. Lamplight glowed suddenly in one of the windows in the rear wall. Four men left the bunkhouse, one of them pausing long enough to shout something back through the open doorway, and stalked awkwardly on their high heels to the corral. They selected horses and rode off to the south. The relief crew. That meant riders would be coming to have their turn at the table. He would have to watch for them, Dan realized.

Minutes dragged into an hour . . . two. The warm sand began to cool, and a faint breeze sprang up out of the east, stirred the trees, and gently shook the brush. Lights in the bunkhouse went out. The cook, finished with his work, walked into the yard, stretched, and headed for the barn, where he would likely engage in a card game or two with the wranglers before he turned in. The riders who were yet to eat would find their meals waiting. So far there had been no sign of them. It was turning into a serious problem for Dan Ricker.

But finally they came loping in, sun-beaten and weary. They turned their mounts in to the corral and made their way to the kitchen. When they had disappeared inside Dan decided it was safe to move. He obtained the sorrel, dropped off the end of the butte, and, circling wide according to plan, came into the brush south of Gorman's house.

There he dismounted. Anchoring the horse, he slipped quietly through the night toward the front of the structure. At the end of the long porch that ran the building's full width, he halted. The windows of the room at the opposite end were alight — and open. He could hear the low mumble of voices, but he could not distinguish the speakers.

He eased in nearer, keeping to the yard and avoiding the wooden floor of the gallery and the possibility of creaking wood when his weight was placed fully upon it. A door slammed somewhere. Ricker froze. Moments later he heard the measured rap of boots crossing the hardpack. He breathed a sigh of relief. It would be the late arrivals, finished with their suppers, heading now for the bunkhouse.

The front door of Gorman's was closed. It stood directly before him across the width of the porch. He waited and listened, striving to determine from the voices just who was in the lighted room. Suddenly a chair creaked noisily. Dan caught the sound of footsteps and sensed, rather than knew, that someone was moving toward the door.

He wheeled and silently retreated to the corner of the building. The door opened. The screen arched outward. Jack Gorman, closely followed by Sandusky, stepped onto the porch.

# CHAPTER
# TWENTY

The two men walked to the edge of the porch, the tips of their cigarettes round, red punctures in the black curtain of night.

Jack said, "We're lining out for town."

Clint Sandusky uttered a small sound of surprise. "Now, hold on, Jack. You know what your pa said."

"Sure I know, but I ain't about to stay holed up here for the next couple of weeks! It's been a month of Sundays since I bellied up to a bar."

Sandusky was quiet for a time. Finally he said, "Maybe so, but your pa sure will do some powerful hell raisin' when he finds out."

"Won't be the first time."

"Could be the last for me. He run me off once. Sure don't want him firin' me again if I can help it. Need this job."

"He won't fire you. I'll see to that. I'll tell him was me who made you come along."

Sandusky flipped his cigarette into the yard. It struck the hardpack and sent up a small shower of sparks.

"I don't know, Jack," he said morosely. "After what happened, could be you ought —"

"Ought to stay put — hang around here close to Pa like I was a runny-nosed kid or something? Why? Burke's dead, and there sure ain't no other lawman going to try anything."

"What about that Ricker?"

Gorman laughed. "If he's able to move after yesterday, I'll bet you won't find him closer'n forty miles on the yonder side of the Pecos. We've seen the last of him."

"I ain't so sure. Looked to me like one of them kind that when somethin' sticks in his craw, he don't quit until he spits it out."

Jack swore softly. "You're a lousy judge of men, Clint. It's even money Ricker's long gone out of this country by now. Anyway, if we run into him, I reckon the two of us can handle him."

Sandusky muttered, "Sure . . . sure." After a moment he added, "What about them Comancheros? Your pa said we —"

"Got away from them once, reckon I can again if they're still prowling around here."

"Might not be so easy."

"Hell! We ain't even sure they're out there! Fincus said him and the boys chased them clear out of sight when they jumped them following Gabe and that herd. I figure they've give it up."

"Sure hope so. I ain't hankerin' to tangle with them."

Dan Ricker, crouched close to the corner of the house, felt his muscles begin to cramp. He steadied himself against the wall and shifted his weight to ease the strain. His foot came up against something, a stone or a piece of wood. A hollow click sounded in the hush.

144

Clint Sandusky spun. "What was that?"

Gorman turned his head and stared into the deep shadows lying along the house. Dan, inwardly cursing himself, waited out the dragging moments. If the two men chose to investigate, his hand would be forced. He would have to fight — and if it came down to that, he would have small hope of taking Jack Gorman. At the first gunshot the entire family — apparently on edge because of the Comancheros, who were still trying to recapture their prizes — would be down on him along with the hired hands. His one chance to get the killer to Canyon City lay in seizing him quietly and quickly and being well on his way before Frank Gorman knew what had happened.

Sandusky drew his pistol and walked toward the end of the porch. If it had been possible, Dan would have pulled deeper into the shadows, but he could not risk it. In the darkness he was certain to stumble against something and create more noise. And edgy as Sandusky was, the puncher would shoot instantly.

It was better to wait, to let Clint move in close, then strike quickly. A sharp blow to the head with a gun butt would fell him. What Jack Gorman would then do was problematical. He could only wait and see.

He crouched lower in the blackness, eyes on the slowly approaching figure of Sandusky. Moving his right hand carefully, he drew his pistol, shifted it about, and grasped it by the barrel. He was trusting to luck that the puncher would not spot him too soon. Jack Gorman's low voice split the hush suddenly.

"Forget it, Clint. Must've been a varmint of some kind. Sure don't hear nothing now."

Sandusky came to a stop. He hung there for several moments, a stooped, threatening shape in the night. Abruptly he dropped his gun into his holster, shrugged, and wheeled about. Ricker sagged against the wall and brushed at the sweat on his face. It had been a tight three minutes.

"Well — you coming along or ain't you?"

Jack's voice was sharp, impatient. Sandusky, again beside him, swore feelingly.

"All right," he said. "Be hell if I do and hell if I don't. Reckon your pa 'druther I'd trot along than leave you go by yourself. Told me my job was to sort of keep an eye on you."

Jack laughed. "Sounds like Pa. Still figures I'm a runny-nosed kid."

"Seems you do get yourself in a powerful lot of trouble. How soon you want to start?"

"Right now. Pa and Amos are already asleep. Yancey's in there reading a book or something."

"How you aim to get by him?"

"Yancey won't say nothing. Probably won't even notice. You get the horses — lead them around the back side of the bunkhouse. Can't take no chances on waking up Pa. I'll get some cash and meet you about a hundred yards out the east road. Understand?"

Sandusky said, "Yeh, I got it." There was a moment of silence, and then the puncher added, "You plumb set on doin' this, Jack?"

A last quarter moon, struggling to break through layers of high, thick clouds, succeeded at that instant. Its pale light spread over the land and brought the two men into more definite focus. Gorman glanced upward.

"Going to be a right fine night for riding. Go on, get started — and don't worry about anything. We'll be back by daylight. Pa won't even know we been gone."

Sandusky muttered something and struck off toward the corrals.

"Easy now," Jack warned. "Don't be stirring up a fuss."

Clint walked on, making no reply. Gorman watched him until he was out of sight; then, pivoting, he opened the door and entered the house.

Dan Ricker's mind worked swiftly. Things were breaking his way; he could think of only one possibility where matters could go wrong — the Comancheros. Evidently Chino and his renegades were still hanging around. He would have to chance encountering them.

He dropped back into the brush and made his way to the sorrel. Halting, he listened. Faint sounds were coming from the corrals. Sandusky was getting the horses.

Dan untied the gelding and led him toward the butte. He did not mount, fearing he might become silhouetted against the skyline and noticeable to Clint. When he reached the first outcropping of rock, he went to the saddle. For a long minute he strained into the night, now soft-silver in the moon's glow. Clint was still at his chore.

Dan rode on. He wanted to be set and waiting when they arrived.

# CHAPTER
# TWENTY-ONE

They were not long in coming.

Dan Ricker, on the saddle, had chosen the black depths of a cedar thicket at the end of a sharp curve in the Masonville road for his position. From that vantage point he could see the moonlit strip of dust for a full fifty yards as it bore straight for him. He had calculated each move carefully; he would wait until they reached the near end of the curve; then he would ride into the open suddenly. Surprise would be his strong weapon. It should be possible to take both Gorman and Sandusky without firing a shot.

He listened to the slow, rhythmic tunk-a-tunk of the approaching horses. Jack was using care. He was holding off until they were a safe distance from the ranchhouse before he put the horses to a lope. Dan drew his pistol and checked the cylinder. It was fully loaded and ready, its action smooth and quiet, thanks to the cleaning and oiling job done by Rufus Coyle.

Coyle . . . Marfa.

His thoughts followed that orderly pattern. He wondered what she was doing at that moment. Probably sleeping, he decided. He hoped she was not worrying too much. There was no need. The way it was all shaping up, things would work out fine.

The riders broke into view at the opposite end of the strip. Clint, head down, slumped on his saddle in glum silence. Jack was humming a tune of some sort, now and then glancing over his shoulder. Dan allowed them to draw near. Suddenly, pistol in hand, he rode from the brush.

"Hold it!" he barked.

Both men hauled to a sliding stop. Their horses, startled, reared briefly, then settled down.

"It's him!" Jack said in an awed voice, peering through the night. "Sure as hell — it's Ricker."

"You're right," Dan replied. "Sit easy and nobody gets hurt. Make a move and I'll shoot —"

"Shoot and be damned!" Sandusky yelled and stabbed for his gun. "I'll be Goddamned if I —"

Ricker's bullet tearing into his heart silenced the rest of his threat. Clint's horse went to its hind legs again and then plunged to the side of the road. Sandusky toppled and fell heavily to the ground.

Within himself Dan was furiously cursing his luck. He had not figured on opposition from either of the men; now the gunshot would arouse the Gormans, put them on the move when they discovered Jack missing. Outwardly, however, he was cool as December wind.

"You want to try me, Jack?" he asked in a low, savage voice.

Gorman was staring at Sandusky's crumpled shape. He shook his head. "No," he muttered, and let it end there.

**149**

Dan moved up, pulled the outlaw's gun from its holster, and thrust it into his own belt. That done, he took a short length of rawhide he had earlier provided himself with from inside his shirt.

"Your hands — stick 'em out."

Gorman delayed briefly, then extended his arms. "You're a damn fool, Ricker," he said, regaining some of his composure. "That shot will have Pa and the boys down on your neck in a hurry. You won't have a chance."

"Seems I remember you saying that before," Dan replied, pulling the thong tight and knotting it securely. He was working fast, aware that Jack was speaking the truth. He must get his prisoner out of the area at once or again face the Gorman clan.

"Still don't get it," Jack mumbled. "Just don't savvy why you're doing this — not being a lawman."

"Like your pa, you'd never understand," Ricker said. "Let's go."

Gorman wheeled about. Suddenly, he drove his spurs into his horse and started back down the road for the ranch. Ricker, on the alert for such, kneed the sorrel into his path and seized the outlaw's reins. Gorman's mount halted abruptly, almost throwing its rider.

"Try that again," Dan said in a low voice, "and I'll blast you off that saddle."

Gorman, recovering himself, forced a laugh. "You don't want me dead. You've got to get me to Canyon City alive and kicking."

"The hell I do," Ricker snarled. "And if I have to shoot you later on to save my own hide, I'll do it. You said it yourself — I'm no lawman, and that's where the difference comes in. I'm not all laced up with a lot of fancy notions about taking my prisoner in alive. I will if I can — but I sure don't have to."

Silenced, Jack Gorman cut back across the road and pointed northward, Ricker no more than a length behind him. They rode at a lope, Dan taking no precaution to hide the sound of their passage, since he deemed it unnecessary. It would be another quarter hour or so before Frank Gorman and his crew reached the bend in the road and found Clint Sandusky's body.

More time would elapse while they searched about for hoofprints that would tell them the exact trail Dan had taken. And by then Ricker figured he and his prisoner would be miles away enjoying a substantial lead.

And they should be able to maintain that lead. The situation was different now. Their horses were fresh, and they had food and water, and there was darkness to mask their course. And he did not have Marfa to consider.

A few minutes later Dan heard the hard, distant drum of running horses. The Gormans were on the move, taking the trail to Masonville. He could visualize them streaming out of the yard of the Double Diamond, thundering off into the night. He could picture Frank Gorman's rage when they found Clint and realized that Jack was again a prisoner on his way to the gallows.

The old rancher would fume and threaten and do his utmost to stop it again; but this time he would fail. This time he would learn that no man was bigger than the law — and that in itself would be partial payment for the death of Ben Burke.

They rode on through the silver-shot night, following a chain of low foothills that flowed in smooth humps across the limitless plains. Twice they came upon sleeping herds. Dan gave them a wide berth. He did not know if it was Gorman stock or not, but he took no chances, carefully avoided running into any of the riders on nighthawk duty.

Several times he again heard running horses, and once he thought he detected someone close on their trail; but no rider materialized out of the darkness, and he dismissed it as imagination and a product of his own wariness.

Shortly after daylight Ricker called a halt to rest the horses and eat. He risked a small fire, using powder-dry wood to avoid smoke, and made coffee. They ate in silence, and when the meal was finished Ricker rose and walked slowly to the horses. He examined them briefly. They were in fine shape. He need not worry about them.

His thoughts came to a full stop. Movement on a ridge far to their right caught his eye. Riders — a half dozen or so. It couldn't be Frank Gorman and his crew — not so soon, and certainly not in that direction. As he squinted at the distant figures, he felt his hopes and confidence drain slowly . . .

The Comancheros.

# CHAPTER
# TWENTY-TWO

Ricker wheeled to Gorman. "Get mounted. We're pulling out."

The outlaw, obviously stalling, shook his head. "Ain't through eating yet."

Impatience ripped through Dan. He pointed to the riders. "They catch up to us it'll be your last meal," he said grimly.

Gorman frowned and got to his feet slowly. "Who's that? Pa'd not be over there."

"Not him. It's the Comancheros."

"Comancheros!" Gorman echoed. "Some of the hands said they'd seen them hanging around. Ain't looking for us. Be the girl they're hunting for."

"Maybe," Ricker said, swinging onto the sorrel. "Don't forget Chino paid for us, too. Could figure we're better than nothing."

The outlaw went to the saddle, and they pulled out immediately. For a good half hour they loped in silence. Dan kept his eyes on the renegades. Chino seemed content merely to stay abreast and not close in from the side. Ricker tried to figure what was in the man's mind, what plan he could be following, and as the miles wore by and the Comancheros held their position, the mystery of it deepened.

Near midmorning they began to pull gradually out of the low area that bordered the foothills and eventually topped out onto a vast, unbroken tableland. Minutes later it appeared to Dan that the Comancheros had begun to draw nearer. He studied them for a time and saw that he was correct; the outlaws were slanting toward them at a long angle. He realized then what Chino's intentions were; he had delayed until they were on the flat where there would be no hills and gullies to provide a hiding-place. Now the Comancheros would simply run them down.

Ricker increased their pace. It might be possible to outrun the renegades, but that was doubtful. Neither Canyon City nor any other sign of human habitation was anywhere on the horizon. Chino had chosen well. Dan glanced to Gorman. His features were taut, strained.

They rushed on, aware of the Comancheros' steady, relentless approach. Dan tried to work out a plan, a means by which they could swerve aside and avoid the oncoming renegades. But interception was inevitable. It would finally come down to a matter of fighting, of trying to hold them off, no matter how he figured it.

He reached into his pocket for the few remaining cartridges he had for the rifle. Pulling the weapon from the boot, he fed them into the magazine. When the time came he would release Gorman's hands and let him use the long gun. Only one thing was in their favor — Chino would want to take them alive.

154

His strategy would likely be to keep moving in, draw their fire in the hopes they would quickly expend their ammunition. To counter that Ricker and Gorman would have to make every shot count, waste none of their bullets. Dan wondered if he could depend on Jack to follow such orders. Or was he likely to panic and bring a sudden end to the chase?

Chino was near enough to be recognizable now. He leaned forward on his horse, quirting the racing animal with a steady back-and-forth lashing. The rest of the renegades were close behind. Dan veered in nearer to Gorman, digging for the knife in his pocket. He paused.

Gorman, turned from him and watching the oncoming riders, suddenly yelled, "They're pulling back!"

Perplexed but relieved, Ricker kept his eyes on the renegades, who were now curving back toward the hills. But there had to be a reason for it. Fresh alarm shot through Dan. Chino wouldn't give up for no cause. He swung his attention to the left, to the broad, somewhat lower plain to their west. He understood then — four riders striking north. He studied them through eyes narrowed to cut down the glare. It was Frank Gorman and his party. Jack's exultant voice broke into his thoughts.

"Pa and the boys, that's it! They've seen them, backed off."

With Gorman were Amos and Yancey and a rider he did not know — Clint Sandusky's successor, apparently. Dan watched them for several minutes while he racked his brain for an explanation as to how they could have not only sliced his lead but actually overtaken him and his prisoner so soon. He backtracked the road the Gormans were following and found the answer. The route he and Jack had pursued along the foothills bowed deeply to the east.

Gorman, knowing the country well and knowing also Dan's ultimate destination, had doubled westward and dropped onto a good direct-line road that led straight to Canyon City. In that one move he had cut miles off Ricker's start.

Dan glanced at Jack's smirking face, then allowed his gaze to shift to Chino and his men, now loping slowly for the hills. He could thank Gorman for that — for delivering them from the Comancheros — but beyond that he was no better off. He now had the rancher and his party to face.

"Be a good time for you to be saving your hide," the outlaw yelled. "Let Pa get on ahead; then you swing back and head south on the road. About your last chance, Ricker."

Dan stared at the distant horizon before them. Thin smudges of smoke hung in the sky. He brushed at the sweat on his forehead, ignoring Jack. Canyon City at last. Maybe he would make it after all.

He glanced into the direction the Comancheros had taken. Chino had not given up entirely, and he would continue to hang around, lurking in the hills. He swung then to Frank Gorman. The rancher puzzled him. He was not turning; indeed, he seemed to be ignoring his

**156**

captive son and the man with him, and with his party he was continuing on.

"Pa won't let you off with no beating this time," Jack warned. "You've crossed him bad. This time he'll fill you full of holes and nail your hide to a tree."

"Like I said before, he's still got to catch us," Ricker replied. "There's only four of them. They can't block all the roads into town."

"The hell they can't!" the outlaw yelled. "Ain't but one way in and one way out of Canyon City. Man's got to go and come at the ends."

That was the answer, Dan realized, recalling what he had heard of the settlement. The town lay in the center of a deep canyon, with entrance and exit only at its ends. There were no approaches from the sides. The story was that a wagon train had once forted up in the depths of the gash to stand off an attack by Comanches. The location had proved so impregnable that many had elected to remain; thus the town had been born.

It was made to order for Frank Gorman. He could lie in ambush at the mouth of the canyon — at each end if need be. No one would be able to pass without his sanction. Further, the people of Canyon City would be totally unaware of what was happening until it was too late.

"Don't be thinking you can swing around to the yonder end," Jack said. "It's a rough ten miles. And when Pa sees you trying it, he'll send Amos and Yancey up there to wait. Give it up, Ricker. You're done."

"Keep riding, damn you!" Dan shouted as Gorman began to pull in.

"Nothing but a dead end for you," Jack protested. "Pa said that — and he'll sure as hell make it so. Call it off while you've still got time."

Ricker's lips pulled into a hard grin. "Suppose I told you it didn't make much difference whether I got by your pa or not? What if I said we'd risk it — gamble on making a run and slipping by. Might work. But if it don't — well, it don't. What would you say to that?"

Jack stared at him. "I'd say you were the biggest damn fool I'd ever run across! And it'd be so — getting yourself blasted for something that was none of your butt-in in the first place."

"Don't forget you'll be right there alongside me, and bullets are blind. So if it comes down to making a run for it, we'll both make it or we'll both be dead."

The outlaw's face was worried, stricken. "Pa'd watch himself, be careful."

"Little hard to do at a time like that. Just wanted you to understand — and if we don't get through you can tell me again what a damn fool I am when we reach hell."

Jack Gorman fell silent, and they continued on at a steady pace. The Gorman party was almost out of sight now, following the road that curved gently westward in its approach to the settlement. They would arrive at the mouth of the canyon a good hour ahead of him, Dan estimated. They would have ample time to lay their trap. The Comancheros had halted, he noted. They were now dim figures on a distant ridge, seemingly content to watch and wait.

Ricker considered the possibility of avoiding Canyon City, of taking his prisoner to some other town. The drawback was apparent. In which direction did another settlement lie? The only one he knew of was Masonville, and it was far to the rear, somewhere east of Gorman's ranch. And there were the Comancheros to consider.

Canyon City was the only answer. If he could make it, his troubles would be over. It was within reach now, and he needed to figure out only one problem — how to get there alive.

Shortly after noon he called a halt for lunch. There seemed no real reason to hurry. They just had to keep moving toward their goal. Jack protested the tightness of his bonds, but Dan refused to listen to the outlaw's grumbling and went about the business of making coffee and sharing the fried meat and hard biscuits in the sack.

As he sipped at his cup of bitter black fluid, Ricker threshed the issue about in his mind. There was a way to beat Frank Gorman, he was sure, if he could just put his finger on it. Everything would not be in the big rancher's favor; there was always a loophole somewhere in the toughest problem — if you could find it.

They finished the meal and pressed on. Around the middle of the afternoon Dan stopped again. The canyon wherein the town lay was evident now. It appeared to rise slightly above the plain in a narrow cleavage, half above the level land, half below.

He could trace the road as it curved to the entrance. Masses of rock and brush were piled on either side, forming perfect cover for ambush. He saw nothing of the Gormans, but they were there, he knew, awaiting only his arrival to show themselves.

Dan allowed his gaze to travel up the sides of the canyon. From the road a man could cut off and make his way to the rim. There was a trail on each side. Once on top, there was no place to go except on across the flat or to the opposite end of the deep slash.

A glimmer of an idea began to shape up in Ricker's desperately working mind. Squinting, he carefully traced the trail on the east slope where it met the entrance to the canyon itself. It was steep and rough. Foot by foot he studied it, pursued it, familiarizing himself with its twists and turns. When he was finished he had a fairly definite understanding of what it was like.

He flung a glance to the east, assured himself that no promise of trouble was forthcoming from Chino and his Comancheros, still on the ridge, then turned to Gorman.

"Use your spurs. We're going in fast."

Jack's mouth dropped open. Disbelief blanked his features.

"You aiming to make a run for it?"

"Mean just that. Figuring on having you locked in a cell before dark."

# CHAPTER
# TWENTY-THREE

They headed for the mouth of the canyon. Dan was gambling heavily on surprise — and the hope that two of the Gorman party, logically now divided and placed at either side of the entrance, would pull out and race for its opposite end when they saw Jack and him apparently moving toward that point.

There was one major source of worry — Jack himself. Forcing the outlaw to do exactly as he was told could be difficult. Aware that he was slated for certain death once in Canyon City, he could prefer to risk a different kind of end at the hands of his captor and make a break for freedom.

It was a very real possibility, and Dan recognized it and sought an answer. One thing was in his favor; a broad streak of cowardice lay in the makeup of the youngest Gorman, and if he ran true to form, he would likely avoid courting death in the hope that something, somehow, would intervene at the last moment to save him. Ricker realized it wasn't much to go on, but it was all he had.

Later, when they paused to rest the horses for the final sprint, Dan took the added precaution of tying Gorman's bound wrists to the saddlehorn. While he was engaged in this security measure, Jack, seemingly still in doubt as to Ricker's real intentions, spoke.

"You actually going to try bustin' by Pa and the others? That what you've got in mind?"

Dan favored the outlaw with a dry smile. "That's it. And while we're talking about it, you do what I tell you, when I tell you — and do it fast."

Recognizing a possible out, Gorman said, "Well, now, maybe I won't."

"Up to you," Dan said, shrugging. "Just keep remembering though that I'll be right behind you with my gun pointed at your back." He finished anchoring Gorman's hands and glanced ahead. The brush and rocks at the mouth of the canyon were more distinct, but there was still no evidence of the Gorman party.

Ricker mounted his sorrel, and they rode on. He picked up the conversation. "You ever see a man with a bullet in his backbone, Jack?"

Gorman frowned. "What's that got to do with me?"

"Plenty. Just want to remind you that it makes a bad cripple of a man. He can't walk, can't even sit down without it hurting like hell. About all he can do is lie around — sort of rot away."

Jack's face was a shade lighter. "Can't see why you're telling me —"

"You can't? Just want you to know what's waiting for you if you don't do what I say. No matter what happens to me, you're done for. Either you'll be dead, or you'll be alive — with two or three slugs in your back. One's bound to smash your backbone, because that's what I'll be aiming for. And at close distance I can't miss."

Jack Gorman made no reply. He rode on, slumped forward over his saddle, chin sunk into his chest. After a time he looked at Dan. There was hopelessness in his features, desperation in his voice.

"Be reasonable, Ricker — make a deal with Pa. I'll do what I can —"

"Too late for that," Dan said, grateful that his purposely grim words had driven home. "We both know it's going to be a showdown — and you're the prize."

The entrance to the canyon in which the town lay took definite form. Dan could see the slight bend in the road as it curved into the canyon and led off down a long grade to the houses and business buildings. The trails rising to the rim on either side were plain also. They looked better than they had appeared before. That gave him some heart.

His eyes probed the brush for the waiting Gormans, but he could not locate them. Back fifty yards or so he thought he could make out the shadowy outlines of a horse hidden in the shrubbery. He could not be certain, however.

He slowed their pace to a trot. The horses were breathing easy and he had no worry as to their condition or their ability to make the fast run he contemplated. He needed only to judge the proper moment to make his move; too soon would allow Frank Gorman and his men time to react; too late would bring him dangerously close.

Ricker studied the land ahead. A few hundred yards farther on there was a slight roll in the ground where

**163**

the plain dipped and sloped off gently to the level of the road. From that point, he guessed, it was a full quarter mile to the mouth of the canyon — and the ambush.

It was the logical spot from which to put his plan into action, Dan decided. He dared get no nearer, for such would place him within rifle range. He slanted a look at Jack, debating the wisdom of telling the man just what he had in mind. After some consideration he ruled against it. Better simply to shout his instructions at the outlaw as the need arose; Jack reacted to and obeyed better under extreme pressure, seeming to do blindly and without question whatever he was told.

They approached the roll in the plain. Again Dan Ricker searched the brush for the Gormans but saw nothing. The rancher and his men were well hidden. Beyond the edge of the canyon, a mile or so within its depth, the town was in view. It was of fair size, Dan noted. A dozen or more buildings frosted the single main street on either side; double that number of residences scattered out behind them.

"Swing right," Dan ordered suddenly. "We're going to the top!"

Jack swerved his horse, a long-legged bay, off the rise and headed up the long grade for the rim of the canyon. Here the ground was still smooth, covered with grass, and the ascent was not steep.

"Use your spurs!" Ricker yelled.

Gorman half-turned on his saddle as though inclined to challenge the command. He took one look at Ricker's grim, hardset face and cocked pistol, and thought better of it. He dug his heels into the bay's flanks and, with the sorrel crowding close behind, increased the pace.

In only moments they were parallel with the opening in the canyon, now a long thousand yards below. Watching, Dan saw Frank Gorman leap into view. He was waving his arms and shouting. Ricker grinned. So far the plan was working well.

Near the top of the slope, he again swung his eyes to the pass below. Two riders, Yancey and the Double Diamond rider he did not know, were on their horses and streaking down the road, heading for the opposite end of the canyon.

Frank Gorman had taken the bait. Seeing Ricker and Jack swing around the entrance where he had laid his ambush, he figured they would try to come in from the far end. Immediately he had split his force in order to guard the other point. Dan smiled again. It was an old trick, as old as war itself — divide and conquer.

"Hold it!" Dan yelled at Jack. "Turn around. We're going down the trail!"

Gorman stared. "I thought you —"

"So did your pa — only we're not! We're taking the trail to the bottom — and we're taking it fast. When we get there, turn the corner and head for town. And Goddamn you, remember I'm riding your tail!"

Dan did not wait for Gorman to move out of his own accord. He wheeled in alongside the bay and slapped it smartly on the rump. The horse leaped forward and started down the trail at reckless speed.

Ricker spurred the sorrel after him. Halfway down he saw Frank Gorman and Amos burst from the brush in surprise. The racket set up by the plunging horses had drawn their attention. Dan, allowing the sorrel his head, drew his second gun — Jack's gun. He snapped two quick shots at the Gormans and watched them duck and scramble for the shelter of the rocks.

Ahead Jack was swaying back and forth on the saddle as the bay struggled to hold his footing. With both hands lashed to the horn, the outlaw could do little but hang on, fighting to hold his seat. Rocks, loose gravel, brush were clattering about him, and Ricker realized it would be somewhat of a miracle if the two horses reached the bottom without falling.

Abruptly they were on level ground. The mouth of the canyon with its broad, dusty road was only fifty feet away.

"Cut right!" Dan yelled.

Jack Gorman seized that moment to muster his one measure of courage. He ignored Ricker's command, kneed the bay to the left, headed for the brush where his father and brother had taken refuge.

"Like hell!" Ricker shouted, and drove his spurs deep into the sorrel's flanks, sent it surging forward.

Broadside to Jack's bay, he veered in. He leaned forward, struck at the horse's head, crowded him hard. The bay, half-wild with fright, swerved back onto the road and raced on for the town.

At that instant Dan saw Frank Gorman and Amos leap from the brush, guns in hand. There was no time to take aim as he wheeled to follow Jack. He snapped a shot with each pistol. He saw the puffs of smoke from Gorman's weapons even as he triggered his own. A slug plucked at his arm, and another screamed off the cantle of the saddle. He saw Frank Gorman sag to one knee.

Ricker fired twice more, both times at Amos, but the man was dodging through the brush, and he could not tell if his bullets had scored or not.

And then suddenly he was out of range, thundering down the road after his prisoner.

# CHAPTER
# TWENTY-FOUR

The sorrel overtook the bay just as it reached the first of Canyon City's buildings. Dan reined in beside Jack.

"Head for the marshal's office!" he yelled.

There were still Yancey and the Double Diamond puncher to be considered. They would have heard the gunfire, suspected something had gone wrong, and wheeled about. These were the critical moments, Ricker realized. He was in between the two groups. Frank Gorman, if he were able to ride, would be mounted and, with Amos flanking him, would come charging in. And if he could not — there was Amos, certainly no less a danger.

People along the sidewalks had stopped and were looking at them with surprised, frowning faces. Others scurried to get out of their way. Ricker's eyes swept the store fronts, searching for the jail. Midway he saw it, a narrow, single-story structure with the faded sign MARSHAL nailed above the door.

He slowed, leaned over, and grasped the reins of Jack's bay. Taking charge of the horse, he angled toward the lawman's quarters. Somewhere farther down the street he heard the quick hammer of hooves. That would be Yancey and his partner. But he had the edge on them now. There were no sounds from the opposite end of the town. He guessed Frank Gorman was having trouble. And either Amos had been hit or else the old rancher was keeping him at his side. It was not ending there, however, Ricker was sure. The Gormans would not quit so easily.

He pulled to a halt in front of the lawman's office. A bearded old man wearing a deputy's star came through the doorway and stopped on the boardwalk. He held a shotgun in his hands.

"What the devil's goin' on —" he began, and then choked off his question as his eyes fell upon Jack. "Where did you get —"

"Later!" Dan snapped, and came off the sorrel. He stepped to Gorman's side and tore at the knots in the buckskin strap that held the killer's hands to his saddle. They came free, and he pulled Jack to the ground and shoved him at the deputy.

"Lock him up — quick!"

"Yes, sir!" the old lawman said, recovering from his surprise. He reached for Jack's arm and propelled him through the doorway into the building. As Ricker stepped up onto the walk and took a stand in front of the door, he heard a hard, metallic clang and the dry grating of a key in a lock. He began to breathe easier.

The deputy pressed up behind him. "What's goin' on? Who're you? How'd you get a hold of Gorman? Where's Burke?"

Ricker grinned faintly despite the seriousness of the moments. "Burke's dead," he replied. "I'll explain the rest later." He glanced down the street and frowned.

What had happened to Yancey and the Double Diamond puncher? He had heard them coming — and then quite suddenly there were no further sounds of them.

"Better get these people out of the way," he said then, aware of the steadily accumulating crowd. "The rest of the Gormans are here. You can figure on trouble."

"Yes, sir," the deputy said again, and started to push by him. He hesitated, hand on the knob of the door. "You want yourself a scattergun? Couple more inside."

"What I got's fine," Dan replied.

The deputy jerked the door shut and stepped out into the street. He spoke a few hurried words, and the gathering began to break up. It was apparent that the citizens of Canyon City knew the Gorman clan only too well. The old lawman returned to the walk and lined up next to Ricker.

"How long 'fore they'll be comin'?"

"Here now," Dan said grimly. "Left two at the south end of the canyon. Was two more at the north side. They started back — heard them coming — then something happened. Don't know where they went."

"Prob'ly circled 'round the back side o' town, figurin' to join up with the others."

Ricker nodded, shifting his eyes to the south. Tension settled over him. "Here they come," he said softly.

They entered the town four abreast, walking their horses slowly. Frank Gorman and Amos were in center, Yancey and the puncher at the flanks. A bloodstained bandana was knotted about the elder Gorman's leg just

**170**

above the knee. His face was set, and there was no admission of defeat in his eyes or in the stiff, arrogant pitch of his head.

They halted in front of the jail, thirty feet away from Ricker and the deputy. A dead hush had fallen over the town.

Frank Gorman, his voice firm, said, "I've come for my boy. I aim to get him."

A hard-cornered, humorless grin pulled at the edges of Ricker's mouth. "Too late, mister. He's in a cell where he belongs — and stays."

"That's what you say. I say —"

"Can't stand getting beat, can you, Gorman?" Dan broke in. "Still won't get off your high horse and admit the law's bigger than you."

"Hand him over!" the old rancher yelled, suddenly furious. "Or by God, I'll tear this town apart!"

"You can try," Dan said quietly. "Jack's responsible now for the deaths of three men. If you want to run the score higher — get at it."

"No, Pa!" Yancey Gorman shouted unexpectedly. "He ain't worth it. Heard you say a dozen times he was born to hang. It's the truth. Face up to it."

Surprised, the rancher swung his glittering eyes to his son. "It's your own blood you're talking about, boy. Your own brother. Makes no difference what he's done, we look out for him."

The old deputy shifted nervously, fingering the hammers of his shotgun. Dan waited out the hushed moments. Yancey Gorman looked down. His moment of boldness was gone.

Ricker said, "Not when it's murder you don't. It's the law's business then."

"We're the law in this country!" Amos Gorman yelled, and whipped out his pistol.

Dan lunged to one side. He snapped two quick shots at Amos, aware in that frightful moment of violence that the Double Diamond puncher was also firing at him.

Ricker felt the burn of a bullet along his ribs. Reaction knocked him off-balance. He went down, going full-length onto the splintery boardwalk. The deputy's shotgun roared, shaking the building. Dan saw the charge slam into the puncher, lift him from the saddle, hurl him backward off his horse. Nearby, Amos lay sprawled grotesquely in the dust.

Guns leveled at Frank and Yancey Gorman, Ricker sat up. Wild, surging fury rocked through him as he stared at the rancher. The crazy, hard-nosed old bastard — when was he going to learn? Trembling with rage, he got to his feet slowly. The toll was up to five now — five men dead because of Jack Gorman. And back of Jack — back of it all — stood Frank Gorman. The father was guilty as the son.

"How about it?" he demanded in a harsh, cracked voice. "You satisfied — or you want more blood?"

Gorman was a transfixed shape in the drifting, coiling smoke as he gazed down at Amos. After a moment he lifted his glance to Ricker. The sharpness had faded from his eyes. Now they were dull — and suddenly very old.

"It's done," he said woodenly. And wheeling his ʼrse about, he headed back down the street.

| | | | |
|-----|---|-----|---|
| APL | | CCS | |
| Cen | | Bar | |
| Mob | | Cou | |
| ALL | | Jub | |
| WH | | CHE | |
| Ald | | Bel | |
| Fin | | Fol | |
| Can | | STO | |
| Til | | HCL | |